BEL

The revised version
Second Edition

By
Clinton Benjamin

Dedicated to the ones who can identify themselves in
one or more ways
with Belinda's story.

Remember,
When the going gets tough,
Don't ever give up.
When hope seems to be lost,
Still hang on.
All cannot be totally lost.
Just have faith in the Lord,
For, life as we know,
Isn't a bed of roses.
It's about winning and losing,
About so many things. Life!

---- Clinton Benjamin

CONTENTS

To my bestie
Happy reading
Clinton

28/05/23

MEETING BELINDA

It had been over seven weeks since our neighbour's niece moved in with her. I wasn't around when her aunt, Lyn, came to introduce her to my mother. Mother said that I was at school. Mother remembered the girl's name quite easily: Belinda! It was also my mother's middle name and she hated it!

"I just don't know why my mother chose to name me Belinda," my mother expressed in a disappointed manner.

I was guilty of being a peeping tom since Belinda moved in next door. It all started one Saturday afternoon, I was in my bedroom looking through that window that faced our neighbour's yard. There, my eyes caught a young lady bathing in the backyard! She was only wearing her underwear and I couldn't resist staring at her. Instantly, I knew it was Belinda!

My mother caught me one day! I was totally embarrassed. She severely warned me not to do it again. She added that I was too young, only fourteen, to be lending my eyes to such scenes because it would only create vulgar thoughts within my mind. She was right about that!

"Whatever you saw, please don't say a word to a soul, or else," she scolded me.

Mother said that everyone in the village knew what type of woman Lyn was and that she couldn't afford getting into a quarrel with her over such a thing. Personally, I wouldn't even be surprised if Lyn was deliberately keeping Belinda away from everyone!

Aunt Lyn was not a bad person overall, but she does have a very sharp tongue and knows when to use it. Apparently, when nearly the entire village was scandalising her husband's name, claiming that she treats him like a dog, she walked from one end of the village to the other, proudly shouting:

"Is grudge some of all you grudge me and my husband!" Until she was out of breath!

And mother also related to me an incident which transpired between Lyn and a woman called White Lily. Apparently, White Lily has two children who lived abroad. White Lily who couldn't read or sign her name, relied on Lyn to do that and other businesses for her. Whenever she received any letters or parcels from her children, it was Lyn who always did the reading and signing for White Lily. Until one day when Lyn was informed that White Lily was telling people that she has been stealing some of her yankee dollars whenever her daughters sent her money.

Mother witnessed the drama between Lyn and White Lily. It happened at the public market one Friday afternoon.

Lyn confronted White Lily about the allegation but although White Lily was denying the accusation, guilt conquered her in the end. And only heaven and the Lord could have saved White Lily that day.

"Buy body lotion for those dry and scaly legs of yours!"

"Never in my life I ever sang with a hymn book upside down, during a church service!"

"If you see your name as big as the court house, you wouldn't know."

"I never went to August school," were some of the strong remarks apparently Lyn peppered White Lily with that day, according to my mother.

"Son, White Lily cried like a child that day and fretting with herself, saying that she was not lucky with people." She definitely was not lucky with Lyn as it appeared.

Finally, I met Belinda for the first time at the library in town. I introduced myself, although I must admit I was a bit nervous. She didn't hesitate to speak with me though. I knew too that she was aware that we are now neighbours.

Belinda looked worried. I could see that something was bothering her. I was curious to find out. I actually came to the library to do some research for a science project which was due tomorrow. Nonetheless, I was quite anxious to find out what was troubling Belinda. By the way, I was only interested in being a listener and a friend to Belinda this time. I was too young to think about having a relationship with her anyway.

Belinda suggested that we find a quiet area which we eventually did. She must have seen something in me that made her opened up to me. Belinda must have believed that she could trust me. She went straight to the point.

"It's my aunt."

"What about her?" I quickly asked.

"A lot of things John," she quickly responded too. She continued.

"That aunt of mine is so strange. At first when I came to live with her, she was the nicest person. Now, all of a sudden, she is giving me such a hard time."

It appeared that Belinda had had some problems at her former home. As a result, her aunt brought her to Ponds to live with her.

"You know John, don't get me wrong as it seemed so strange that I am relating my problems to someone of your age," she paused.

"I feel the same way too," I replied, "But I think it's okay to talk to me."

"I have had so many problems in the past and still do. Sometimes I wish I was never born!"

"No, please Belinda, don't ever say that!" I politely advised her. "I understand and I hope the very best for you. At least, everyone deserves a chance in life, regardless of their circumstances or situations."

Having said those words made me felt like I have known Belinda for a long time. I felt like a brother to Belinda. No doubt, she and I would become long lasting friends.

Belinda expressed the struggles she has faced in life and how everyone in her family made her feel like a failure, no matter how hard she tried. Telling her story, she began to cry. I was carrying a handkerchief, so I offered it to her. Her face had become a running river from the constant tears that fell from her eyes. Still, I encouraged her to cheer up.

"Come on Belinda, don't ever give up on life. Who knows, your time to be successful could happen soon."

"You don't un-understand," she slightly stammered. "I've tried my best, but my family continues to tell me that I am a failure. And that really hurts."

Belinda also confided in me that did not complete high school. That she said has caused her to worry a lot too.

"I wanted to become an English teacher," she informed me.

"Belinda," I interrupted. "It's not too late. It might not be easy, but it is possible. I know of an organization that might be able to help you with one of its training programs.

"Oh, John, God must have sent you," Belinda responded with excitement in her voice while patting me on the shoulder.

Although she had stopped crying, the look on her face showed her suffering. Having listened to all that she poured out of her heart, I knew I would truly help her the best way that I could. Of course, I am still a student, unemployed and have problems of my own to deal with. But moral support and encouragement would mean a lot to someone like Belinda. I liked her before we even spoke. While I should confess she has a beautiful face and personality, I have come to like her in a different way. She is a few years older than me and I have also told myself that my future lady would not be older than me. Belinda and I would always be like brother and sister. I could almost bet my life on that!

Belinda picked a white piece of paper from between the pages of the book lying in front of her on the table. She handed me the piece of paper and said confidently, "See, I've been writing some poems. What do you think?"

I read two of her poems and although I am not an expert, I immediately realised her potential.

"Not bad at all, Belinda. In fact, I am very impressed with this particular one:"

> She could be a happy girl
> In this world:
> She could smile much more
> If she is told,
> How well she's appreciated-
> To be loved and not hated.
> She could excel, she could tell
> She'd do very well
> If someone cares, if someone shares
> The key to overcome fear,
> The way to see life
> Without much spite.
> If only you know Belinda

You'd understand what it means:

TO SUFFER!

"Beautiful Belinda." The words in that poem are so strong.

"Thanks, I haven't had such positive comments from anyone in a very long time. You really made my day John," she commented.

From the smile on her face, I know she meant what she said. It was the first time she smiled since we had been talking. She then looked at her watch and immediately her face registered a great shock.

"Is there something wrong Belinda?" I questioned out of concern for her.

"Oh, my God!" She breathed faster and said, in a panic-stricken voice "Both of us got so involved in our conversation that I completely forgot to check on the time. I have to go home to prepare dinner. My aunt is going to kill me"

"Tell her you were at the library," I suggested to Belinda.

"My aunt doesn't believe anything I say. She calls me a liar," she responded, so sadly.

"I am so sorry for you Belinda." Anger suddenly rose in me, thinking about the way Belinda's aunt has been treating her.

"It's okay," she said hesitantly. "Look, I have to go now. Depending on the outcome with my aunt, I should be able to return to the library in a few days," she tried to assure me.

"I'll try and get information on those programs for you," I reminded Belinda.

Belinda shook my hand and then hurriedly picked up her belongings and disappeared. Immediately, a sad feeling came upon me. I never imagined that I would ever meet someone who was hurting so deeply inside as Belinda. I remembered wishing that I had a job or enough money to help her to run away to a better place. Even though she is still a young girl, she has such a warm heart and definitely very intelligent. She should not have been suffering like that. In fact, no one should.

I became so emotional thinking of Belinda's trouble that I couldn't concentrate any longer on my research. All I wanted to do now was to go home, tell mother of Belinda's troubles and say a special prayer for her. I believe too that Belinda has more on her mind and would soon tell me more.

Mother also felt badly about the way Belinda is being treated by her aunt after I related everything Belinda told me at the library.

"Poor child," mother remarked. She continued: "But Lyn doesn't like to listen to anyone. I wouldn't want to be the one to talk to her about her ill treatment towards her niece. Besides, that's sensitive family matter, delicate and personal. Let's just pray that Lyn would open up her eyes and realize that her niece is suffering emotionally and needs he support. From what I heard, Belinda's mother could also be considered reckless and unconcerned for her children wellbeing. God forbid!" mother exclaimed with a hint of anger, understandably.

" I would never leave my children to suffer in this world, no matter what. I'll sacrifice for them because it was I who brought them into this world."

Mother really got caught up in the very unhealthy news of Belinda and her plight.

11

"Lyn knows that the bible talks about," 'suffer not the children...'bring them up in the right way.'

My mother isn't a christian, but from observation she is conscious of Christ's existence.

We prayed together, asking the Lord to intervene...to allow Lyn to see the right way in bringing up an already heartbroken young girl who happens to be her niece. Who seems innocent to many situations in life. I also thanked God for my mother who's thrown some licks on my bottom when I did wrong things, but she never abused the situation. My father ran off to somewhere in the world and left her alone to fend-to provide a livelihood for both of us. And I have seen her crying. I heard her pleaded to God, to carry me safely to and from school. And when I caught pneumonia last year and almost died, it was those last words she uttered to me at my bedside in the hospital that brought me back on my feet again.

"You know that your mother wants to see you around. You can't leave her now. She's gotten so much accustomed to her little angel that she couldn't live without him. I already prayed to God and He promised to bring you back to me. He will bring you back to me.

And the tears she tried to hide fell on my chest as I laid on my back, very weak but trying hard not to let my mother down.

If Belinda had a mother, an aunt like my mother then I would not have felt so worried for her. So mother and I prayed to the Lord that Belinda would see better days soon. We prayed for her aunt as well. That she would see that she's breaking her niece's heart before it's too late.

BELINDA'S STORY: A CRUEL PAST

I grew up on the southern side of the island in a village called Brookes, about half and hour's ride by bus from the city. I lived with my grandparents, along with my two brothers, two sisters and two uncles. My mother, Bertha, lived with us at one point but she left for a neighbouring island called St Thomas when I, her eldest daughter, was around nine years old. Bertha's mother and my grandmother, Juanita, eventually told me and my siblings when we kept asking for our mother that our mother apparently went away with some yankee fella.

Our grandmother hinted a few times too, that if that was the case, why her daughter never wrote nor even sent a dime in the mail. But Juanita never minded. She loved all of her grandchildren and she was especially fond of me. She often reminded me that I was a duplicate of her mother's features, especially when I smiled!

"You look so much like my mother Edna," my grandmother usually expressed to me.

Though food and money were scarce in the home, grandma managed to provide something on the table for us to eat, at least twice a day. To this day, I wished grandmother was still alive because things would have been much different. For one thing, I would have completed high school. Grandma was always instrumental in seeing that our homework was done. She encouraged me and siblings to read a lot of books when they were afforded to us. She always boasted to her friends that one day, there would be a lawyer and a doctor in the family.

And oh, if only her wish would come true! She constantly reminded her grandchildren that one day things would change for the better and now was the time to prepare for such a change. Sadly, it seemed like everything went from good to bad when our beloved grandmother passed away.

I was thirteen years old. Everything really changed, and fast! I remembered that sad day when grandmother suddenly fell ill. Grandpa had sent for the village nurse, but grandma had already passed away when she arrived.

Post- mortem revealed that grandma died from natural causes. Everyone at home felt her death. Grandpa took it particularly hard and sought refuge in alcohol. My uncles followed suit.

The day of the funeral was the saddest moment of my young life. The fact too that mother never turned up for the funeral added to all that sadness. We later found out that she wanted to get her American papers so badly that she refused to leave St Thomas despite her mother's death because it would jeopardize her chances. Everybody in the village had a lot to say. Some even remarked how worthless our mother was and that she only did her family a favour

by not turning up for the funeral. Others blasted her for abandoning her children and never had the decency to send a little yankee dollar home for them.

Grandfather mentioned that his wife, our adorable and lovable grandmother, requested to be buried in the grave of her parents.

"She always brought that up," I overheard grandpa telling our uncles one evening when they were discussing the funeral arrangements. His voice bore grief. Though I was still quite young, I was old enough to feel the blow of grandma's untimely death knocking me to the ground. That same night, grandpa took another shot of some local rum and then put out the oil lamp in the house. It would be another uncomfortable night; to be afraid and to be haunted. I was tempted to say a prayer. I recalled one that our deceased grandma had taught us. My eyes were wide opened in the darkness. Silence stole the hour, except the sound or snoring that was coming from one or two persons in the house and the organised sound of crickets on the outside. My little heart was pounding fast and my eyes withdrew tears. I fought with the reality that grandma was no longer alive. Dead to the world. I remembered rising from my lowly bed and knelt on my knees, whispering a sound that came to my mind in the dark:

> The love of God
> He died for us,
> The love of God
> Can make us glad
> When we are sad,
> Praise ye Jehovah
> Hallelujah, Hallelujah!

I returned to my humble bed and meditated on this prayer:

> "Dear God, if you could bring back our grandma,
>
> you would make me the happiest little girl in Brookes
>
> village. Grandma is thinking about us-You know she
>
> was everything to us and we will miss her badly. Dear
>
> God, Please bring her back to us........"

Grandpa had drunk again. He was stone drunk and couldn't even walk. He even peed on himself. He was lying flat on the floor in the bedroom. His eyes were red like the devil's, although I have never seen him and didn't wish to. I was only using an expression I heard before.

"You miss your grandma, eh?" asked grandpa in an unsteady voice that was threatened by tears. I was right.

"Oh how I miss my wife. Look at me now. I can hardly take care of myself." Grandpa sounded and looked weak both in body and in spirit. The alcohol was strong on his breath as he spoke. It was unbearable and too painful for me to witness.

"You don't have to drink rum grandpa," I suggested in a shaky voice.

"I know, but what's the use? My wife is dead and I am so weak, so weak..."

Grandpa cried so much that he lost his voice that day. He was soon fast asleep, his mouth wide open, showing missing teeth from his upper and lower gums.

The transistor radio was playing. The words of 'show me the way...' caught my attention as the singer sounded like she was looking for guidance from some source. The batteries in the radio were also having their last moment of life. Still, I hummed to the unfamiliar tune, thinking too that I needed someone to show me the way. Grandma wasn't around anymore.

It only took me a few months before I realized that my only hope had gone from this world with the untimely death of my grandmother. Our home wasn't the same anymore. I missed those times when our grandmother used to tell us stories of long ago. I missed how she used to sing to us, combed our hair and read the bible to us each night before we went to bed. Though we lacked many basic necessities in life, our home never lacked love and care, especially from our grandma.

During school holidays, our grandparents used to take us to a place called Valley where many villagers owned plots of land on which they planted vegetables and fruits to sell at the city market on Saturday mornings. Grandpa had a donkey named Barnard. Whenever we went to Valley, everyone except granny got a ride on Barnard, en route.

Grandpa treated Barnard like a king. I remembered only one mishap that involved myself and my two brothers. Andy convinced Jason and me to untie Barnard while grandpa was on the other side of Valley. Grandpa, who was picking peas, was not paying attention. Andy knew it was a perfect moment for us to have a short ride on Barnard. We did but it resulted in a little bit of disaster. During the course of the ride with all three of us on the donkey, Andy forced Barnard to move with more speed. The donkey galloped and before I knew it, Jason and I were on the ground! Luckily, we fell upon plenty of grass but while Jason escaped injury, I broke my left hand and bruised my right knee. Andy managed to control his balance on the donkey so like Jason, he also escaped injury free. However, he was given a very stern warning by our grandmother. She told him that he could have gotten us killed. I was really frightened over the whole incident and swore I would never ride on a donkey again and haven't since.

"But Andy, what got into your head?" asked grandma while looking at him with some very serious eyes.

We went to the community clinic for someone to look after my hand and bruises. Afterwards, grandma took care of me at home with remedies from the backyard. She told me that God saved our lives and I was sure that she was right about that.

Grandma was such a sweet person. Today, I keep wondering why none of her children possess any of her qualities. They were all so bad, especially my mother. And grandpa was a good man too. Only the death of his dear wife changed him a bit. He followed her to her grave exactly one year, one month and one day after her death.

Grandpa came down with a terrible fever that lasted for many weeks. He became very weak and had to stay in bed day and night. Then stopped eating altogether. During the nights, his temperature rose and his sweat soaked his bed.

"I am going to see my wife soon," he used to say to any visitor who dropped by to see him, in a lonely and weary voice that spoke death's arriving soon. Soon to his door.

It was uncle Jim who announced his death one afternoon while we were helping uncle Arthur to feed the pigs. His death was expected but we still had to grieve over it. Grandpa was a member of some organisation until his death. And that organisation took care of most of his funeral expenses.

Our mother did show up her for her father's funeral. It was an embarrassment because nobody noticed her. Even her sister, aunt Lyn gave her a tongue-lashing.

"Papa wanted to see you when he was alive, not when he is dead," aunt Lyn reminded my mother with a touch of sarcasm to it.

"Oh, Lyn, you are the greatest daughter. You have no idea how I wanted to come earlier on but I couldn't. Besides, I never talked back to papa, have you ?" my mother responded with her dosage of sarcasm too.

Aunt Lyn got up from the chair in such a rush and rage and threw her hands in the air as if she was signaling victory of some sort. It was the very opposite outcome because mother approached her like a peacemaker and remarked to her sister:

"Those hands of yours are useless. I only came home to see papa get buried, not to fight."

Aunt Lyn's face turned from a sour expression to sudden exposed guilt.

I could see that somehow, she felt embarrassed in the end. That in the midst of a death in the family, two sisters were at war with each other. I was glad it ended up peacefully. To be honest, I got a scared about it at first. Both sisters were capable of behaving badly. Mother has a small mark in the middle of her forehead. She and my aunt were apparently fighting over a very simple matter: a fried dumpling. Mother wasn't ashamed to talk about it. In fact, she told us that her sister used a fork and punched her over forehead because she didn't hand over the last fried dumpling she had on her plate, one day when they were having their dinner. It happened when mother was around fifteen years old. It wasn't a big mark but because she is somewhat brown-skinned, the little mark is still visible but not an ugly sight to say the least. One would have to be looking closely at her face to notice the mark.

"And mama beat her little behind like it was a drum! When mama was done with greedy Lyn, she couldn't sit down and I was so glad about that!" mother said to us without restriction. But she cautioned us not to ever talk about that incident in our aunt's presence especially.

Aunt Lyn took up her handbag and quietly walked out of the house without uttering another word to anyone, which was a great surprise knowing the character of my aunt.

Mother promised that she would never leave us ever again, but only four days after grandpa's funeral, she left us sixty American dollars with her eldest brother, Jim. She gave each of her children a kiss on the cheek and promised us that she would be back in a week's time and left us in uncle Jim's care. Mother told us that she was returning to St Thomas to finalize certain things, after which she would return to look after us.

We believed her and we anxiously awaited her return. Regardless of what everyone else were saying about our mother, she remains our mother and we really needed her, even more than before. We have no father presence in our lives. Mother has never spoken of him.

But mother did return six months later. Her arrival was greeted with the news that Andy had been sent to prison for having broken into a white lady's place in the next village. Mother simply remarked that she was sick and tired of dealing with Andy. Like, really? What a blatant lie! She was never around to teach us right from wrong and she never had to deal with Andy's changing behaviour. And apparently, my mother was giving the impression that she has been around and had been an influence in our young lives. Spare me the details Miss Bertha Prince! You couldn't careless with what goes on in your children's lives. You had other things on your mind, like earning yankee dollars for yourself and yourself alone. I know that my brother Andy isn't angel, but he also has been feeling the absence of a mother-father figure in the home. Love, care and guidance are what we are crying out for mother!

So Andy became restless and unruly and would not go to school. He eventually found the wrong type of friends and wasn't coming home until the wee hours of the morning. My uncles had problems of their own, so dealing with my brother Andy was the least of their concerns. They just did not care that Andy was drifting with the wrong winds, so he got worse.

Andy and I get along well. He has been telling me that no one really cares for us. My already fragile and poor little heart was broken again when my brother said those words.

Though mother had been away for so long and never seemed to have cared for us, we were still happy that she had decided to stay at home. Things seemed better because she bought the groceries, school supplies and clothing which we desperately needed. I was tired of the painful remarks our neighbours and school peers made from time to time, and worse seeing my young siblings returned from school stained with tears and fears. Two nasty remarks were,' we should be glad that our mother had returned from St Thomas to fill our hungry bellies and 'that our mother must have begged all of St Thomas for the money to clothe our naked backs.' It goes to show how people can be so heartless and insensitive. And sometimes I wished I was a bad girl and just tell those concerned to 'piss off!' or 'you should mind your own business!'

Mother made some repairs to the house and added an extra room. There were already too many of us living in the two- bedroom house. Some of us had to sleep on the floor. The extra room was very much welcomed.

I began to love my mother for the first time. I was getting the impression that she wanted to make up for all the lost years she was away from us. At least, that's what I thought at first. I don't know what had gotten into our mother's head five months after she came back from St.

Thomas. All of a sudden, she was leaving us to attend parties and shows. You name it and she was there. Once again, she was paying less attention to us and regrettably my opinion of her was changing. Sometimes I would hate her so much and another time, I thought I still loved her.

Quite often, she would return home the next morning after her night fetes. There were a few times when she didn't even bother to return home until days later. Meanwhile, our uncles became less concerned about us. I began to skip school to become a mother, a father and a sister to my little brother and sisters. Whenever I complained to mother about her behaviour and treatment towards us, she would threaten to break some part of my body if I didn't stop bugging her. One day, she slapped my youngest brother on the face and ordered him to shut up at once just because he asked her why she was not spending time with us. I couldn't hold back the tears. She demanded that I stop crying or she would give me a real reason to cry.

People started to gossip again but my mother didn't care. She started smoking and was wearing the latest fashions while her children continue to suffer. The neighbours labelled her a prostitute and a vagabond. They kept saying she was a disgrace to her children and thank God her parents were not alive to see her worsening behaviour.

My uncles were unconcerned about their sister's behaviour. They said nothing to her just aunt Lyn showed some concern. She came about once or twice and told her sister to slow down, that the world wasn't running away from her. She reminded her sister to act like a mother and look after her kids or they would grow up to hate her. Mother became very upset and told her sister that it wasn't her fault that she was unable to have children. Aunt Lyn stormed out the house, pointing her middle finger in the air and towards mother, and told her to stick it where the sun never shines!

It was rumoured that mother was seeing a one-eyed married man who had a business in town. People were saying that they would never neglect their children for a married man, but evidently, mother was doing just that.

Helen or Gossip Stick as she is popularly known in the village, tried to make things worse by apparently got in touch with the one-eyed man's wife and informed her of her husband's infidelity with mother. As bad as this was and coming from me being a teenager, I sensed Gossip Stick didn't like my mother and was also jealous of her. Now what my own observations and thoughts, Gossip Stick is fat and greasy looking. She has very long black hair but never kept it well. Worse of all, she was very black skinned (tar baby) and rumour was brewing that she has been trying to bleach her entire body, God knows how long now! Hardly any improvement has been noticed, simply because she is a tar baby! And foolish me think that chlorax could augment the bleaching process for her quite easily! She'd get a whiteness that she didn't want. Hahaha!

Orvilles's wife couldn't be bothered about the rumour since apparently she was more interested in her husband's money. It seemed like all of them were in the same boat; Orville

is having affair with that mother of mine and his wife was having an affair with a cousin of her husband. I overheard Gossip Stick telling someone one day when I quietly walked in the corner shop. May God have mercy upon them all!

My time at Brookes was hard enough already but there were other problems besides those of our mother. Certain events happened back then that still traumatize me to this day.

I will never forget that day. It was a Friday and for some reason, I didn't go to school. Everyone was out except my eldest uncle, Jim. I had taken a bath and had gone into the bedroom to get dressed. The bath towel was still wrapped around me because I was looking for something light to wear given it was very hot that day. The temperature soared to nearly one hundred degrees Fahrenheit.

I was very startled when I turned around and saw uncle Jim standing at the bedroom door, staring suspiciously at me. I thought he was out in the backyard chopping pieces of wood, where I had last seen him. But no, he was in the room with me. I had no idea how long he had been there or what he wanted. I, in a panicked voice asked him what he was doing in the room and requested if he could give me some privacy knowing that I had not dressed yet. I remember his exact words: "What you got to hide, eh?"

As he said those words, he quickly pulled the towel from around me and exposed my nakedness. I was shocked in disbelief and was about to scream ,when he cautioned me to be quiet. He said he wasn't going to hurt me. I begged him not to do any unkind thing to me.

He then locked the bedroom door and then cautioned me to be quiet, I suspected what he was up to but I couldn't believe that such cruel indecency was about to happen between an uncle and his niece. I pleaded and begged him once more not to do anything horrible to me. But all my so called uncle replied was, "Just relax, uncle won't ever hurt you."

My voice and breathing were unsteady as I remembered faintly crying:

"You're not supposed to do that uncle Jim!" But he paid me no mind.

"I will take my time Bee. Just take it easy sweetheart," I recalled my wicked uncle saying, in a voice that suggested that I had nothing to fear. That I was apparently in safe hands. It was unimaginable to think that my uncle had the heart in doing such evil thing to his niece.

When unzipped his pants, I almost fainted. It was abundantly clear what he was going to do, He forced his way on top of me and satisfied his pathetic desires while leaving a permanent stain of fear on my life. He said we should act like nothing happened. He warned me severely that I should never mention what happened between us to anyone. He even told me that he would buy me anything I wanted.

I cried and cried and I told myself that I was going to tell someone about it. Maybe aunt Lyn. But I never did.

> Fighting the pains of my inner being
> Wondering what life would have been:
> If I was wrong.....................
> If I was strong......................

Fighting the tears in my eyes,

Knowing it was all wrong..........

Knowing I am not strong,

Fighting for words,

For comfort.

I never felt the same again. Sometimes I would unexpectedly burst out crying when that wicked moment revisited me. One day at school, my teacher realized that something was wrong with me. She told me that I could talk to her if I wanted to but I never took her up on that offer.

Teacher Esther requested that I stay back in class after school one Wednesday afternoon. She pleaded with me to tell her what's wrong with me. She even offered to buy me lunch for the rest of the week. She might have thought that hunger was a part of the reason why I was showing a sulky face these days.

"But it was much more than that teacher Esther. You really don't know what is going with me."

Even my youngest uncle asked me on several occasions if I was alright. I lied to him out of fear and told him that my mother's neglect was bothering me. Although I was desperate to tell someone about what that wicked uncle Jim did to me, it was very hard for me to do so.

The pain of neglect and the lack of a mother and father guidance grew to be a heavier burden in my mind. If my mother had been around to care for us, her heartless brother might not have had the chance to rape me. Mother made us all afraid of her. It was difficult to speak with her. Living in poverty was one thing but to live also with disrespect, lack of love and care from my family has had a serious effect on me.

Like memories of wasted years

A mother neglected her babies.

Oh look at their poor innocent faces!

Being destroyed by their own families.

They have no help.....

No wings to fly.......

Those innocent faces are crying,

They're crying for a real life:

Help us please!

Uncle Jim or the wicked bastard as I referred to him , didn't stop sexually molesting me. He did it again. And a third time. I was further reduced to nothing and felt more humiliated. I was being taken advantage of and I swore that I must tell someone. My hurt was both mental and physical. Nightmares became nothing unusual for me and I also feared getting pregnant by my uncle, not to mention at such a young age.

That bastard had no regard or respect for himself much less to me. Where was his heart and conscience? Possibly underneath the sole of his feet! With all the problems that were already prevalent in the home and in our lives, how could that bastard be so wicked to me? My heart was heavy, filled with hatred for my family especially uncle Jim. I hated my mother and I regretted being born into such family!

Why do you let their little hearts moan?

Why do the children think they're alone?

They're tired of asking the same questions:

Where's our mother and father?

We are hungry. Cool. Afraid.

Please hold our hands,

Give us a smile...........

Don't you know little children

Have deep wounds on the inside?

I literally wanted to kill Jim. I couldn't stand looking at him anymore. He kept acting as if nothing happened. For that reason alone, I was completely torn apart. I wasn't able to concentrate on my schoolwork. There was too much on my mind. Too much!

I had already advised my two sisters to tell me everything that went in the house in my absence. I was particularly concerned that uncle Jim, the bastard might think he could also sexually abuse them. I certainly didn't want my sisters to also fall victims to their perverted uncle.

God must have given me the strength to carry on. What I really wanted God to give me, was the courage to speak to someone about my hurt. I couldn't bear the burden of that suffering within me anymore. It was too heavy.

I don't know whether or not a guilty conscience had begun to challenge my mother, for on that day, she came into the kitchen and said, "Bee, the children said you don't look happy these days. Are you feeling sick?"

My heart pounded. I was taken aback by my mother's unexpected and bold initiative to inquire about one of her children's feelings. Before I could reply, I was in tears. Mother hugged me and calmly said the nicest things to comfort me. To me, it was like a miracle. As we held each other, I realized that my mother was high from smoking marijuana. It was strong on her breath. But it didn't matter to me. I knew it was the perfect opportunity to let her know what had happened and the pains I feel inside. I was also grateful that only my mother and I were at home that day.

"Speak to me, my child," my mother said in the most commanding, comforting yet confident manner, which only a mother possesses in moments like that. I went straight to the point.

"Uncle Jim did something to me, mother."

"Did what to you Bee?" questioned my mother. I could feel her voice slightly raised.

"You know what a husband and wife do in bed. It was awful and he did it more than once," I bravely disclosed to her.

"Jesus Christ!" my mother exclaimed frantically. "How could Jim do such a thing to you?" She held her head with both hands as if she wanted to take it off her own body. "I thought that I could trust him," she tearfully murmured.

"He is the oldest brother and should have shown some responsibility instead he abused his power. I cannot imagine this." Mother was furious.

The moment mom talked about responsibility, I was convinced she was expressing her own guilt too. She definitely had herself to blame too! If I were to have graded her for parenting, I would have graded her very low.

I was soaked in tears but relieved that I finally told someone. Mother swore that she was going to kill her brother. She had already sharpened one of her papa's old cutlasses. She screamed at the top of her voice. She swore so much that the neighbours came out to see what was the matter. I was ashamed and afraid that they all would start point fingers at me. Despite my fear, I grew stronger and urged mother to calm down. She didn't listen . Instead, she carried on louder.

One neighbour shouted angrily, "What sick man Jim is. If it was my daughter, I would have killed him and let the law deal with me!"

Uncle Arthur finally arrived and couldn't believe what he was told. I have never seen him that angry. For the first time, he blamed his sister, my mother of course.

The house was filled with noise and confusion. And no matter how my mother reacted to my revelations about uncle Jim, no matter how uncle Arthur promised to be there for me from now on, not one of them could heal the emotional and physical wounds , the damage done to me by their brother. I blamed them all. Where was mother when we were growing up and needed her? Running here and there like some wild coot, of course! She had practically neglected us. Why now was she acting like she'd been a good mother? I wanted to tell her that but it would have made matters worse. There was already too much infightings going on. I also didn't want to hurt the feelings of my younger siblings. They were already crying and clinging on to me instead of their unprized mother or uncle. I have been with them from the beginning and love them very dearly.

Uncle Jim must have gotten the news because he never came home that day. In fact, he never came back home at all. We eventually learned that he migrated to a neighbouring island.

Meanwhile, aunt Lyn came to the house the next day. After I disclosed her brother's cruelty to me, she was steamed with anger. She blamed her sister as well. She even threatened to call the police. Somehow, uncle Arthur persuaded her not to do so since it would add more fuel to the fire. Mother just sat in the rocking chair in the kitchen staring at everyone and not saying a word as if she had just lost it.

Aunt Lyn decided to take me to a doctor to have what she termed as 'a wash-out', so I wouldn't be pregnant. Although I did that , I still felt uncleaned and robbed of my childhood's innocence. Just the thought that I was sexually abused by a relative who should have known better. It's been hard facing the reality of it. Believe you me.

> For whatever life is worth,
>
> I never wanted to feel such hurt,
>
> Never want to feel alone.......

Never want to walk alone......

Aunt Lyn took me under her wing. I left Brookes and took up residency with her at another village called Ponds. Mother must have changed from the incident. She promised to be there for her children from now on.

She claimed that Jason, Samantha and Kizzy would have her undying attention. Andy and I would not experience her undying attention because we no longer lived with her. Andy, when released from prison, never bothered to return home. I am certain he was angry that no one

visited him while he was in prison. Maybe mother went once or twice, but that was it.

Reality was sinking in. I could feel the root of it. I was going to miss my little brothers and sisters. I wish we were all going to the same place. I sensed that link of friendship that we had would end. Mother had planned to return to St Thomas and take them along with her.

As I said goodbye to them, the tears streamed down my cheeks like raindrops and like never before. It was like a storm that had just arrived and would not go away soon.

"I love you and I will come back to see you all soon," were the last words I said to my beloved ones before I walked out the house where I spent almost all of my life. I followed aunt Lyn to the bus stop where we would take a bus to Ponds.

Memories of Brookes flooded my mind while I sat beside my aunt on the bus. Most of the memories were cold but there were some good ones too. Most of the good ones were of my grandmother and her hope for all of her grandchildren. When there was nothing to eat, grandmother came forward with tears, brought us in a circle and said, " Never mind children, God will not let you suffer for too long. She pointed towards me, "One day you will know what I was talking about. Out of the five hungry eyes that stared vacantly at our granny, mine were the only ones that shed more tears. My younger siblings were too innocent to understand. But that day, I shed tears for all those memories and the thought that I could only hope for a better life with my aunt.

AUNT LYN

Living with my aunt wasn't that easy. Instead of accomplishing anything worthwhile, I only added frustrations to my life months after I moved to Ponds. Aunt Lyn was good to me in the very beginning. I desperately wanted to finish my high school education. My aunt was so certain that I would get into the high school in her area so she went ahead and got a transfer from the school I previously attended. The process was straightforward and in the end, for whatever reason, I didn't get in. Apparently, my aunt mentioned that she was tired running back and forth, here and there and not getting anywhere in the end. So, she gave up. She tried subsequently to get me into a vocational school, but that too did not materialize. Without my aunt's help, I was hopeless. So eventually I stayed at home , became a housemaid and according to my aunt, a burden to her!

My aunt had changed from the woman I knew when I lived at Brookes. I have become so disappointed in her and slowly came to realize that these days, she only has a cold shoulder for me to lean on.

When my aunt came home one afternoon with tears in her eyes and a sad face, I knew something had turned sour for her. She had been working as a housemaid for a Syrian family for the past seventeen years. That same day when I suspected she did have any good news to share, I was right. The Syrian family had informed her that they would be moving back to Syria in four weeks, That meant she'd be soon out of a job. Understandably, she was saddened and made nervous by the news. It was the only job she ever had.

"Go and get me some brandy with ice! I need to calm my nerves," was the first thing she demanded from me.

I was shocked. I'd never seen her drank alcohol before, unless it was a beer but then again it was only on special occasions.

" Aunt Lyn, are you ...?"

"Save your words child," suggested my aunt bluntly before I completed the question to her. She knew what I was going to ask her and I suspected she wasn't in any mood for questions.

I got her what she requested. She finished the drink in just two gulps and demanded a refill. Seeing my aunt this way was deeply shocking to say the least. She just sat on a chair in the living room talking to herself and crying as if the world had just ended and she had been told that she was destined for hell! I couldn't comprehend why she was making her blood pressure rise so unnecessarily. Yes, she'd be out of a job soon but she hadn't lost everything. She still has her husband to support her and they seemed to have a good relationship.

I offered her dinner, which she took and looked at disdainfully. With my aunt's current mood, I still gathered enough courage to find out from her if there was anything wrong with the food.

" I hope you didn't use up all my chicken and since when did you become the mistress of the house," she unreluctantly answered.

I couldn't believe what was happening. It was not the first time I'd cooked for my aunt. She often complimented my cooking on several occasions. So I was very much surprised to hear her moaning about the food and all that. She is drunk and I am also aware that she is upset about the fact that she would be out of a job within a few weeks. That doesn't give her any valid reasons to take out her frustrations out on me. I would now say less and only respond if and when she asks me a question.

I must admit though that the 'Abduls' had been good to her. She always spoke well of them. I actually went to their home once to assist my aunt with her work. To be honest too, they were really nice to me. Sometimes when my aunt worked late, Mr Abdul would bring her home. He would drop her off in front of the house and waited until she got inside before he waved bye to her and drove off. And every public holiday, she was certain of getting goodies from the Abduls'. It is possible that my aunt was invaded with all those memories and reflections and was reacting the wrong way.

After three glasses of brandy, my aunt was completely knocked out. She did eat all of the dinner before she passed out on the chair. She was now fast asleep and now snoring like a pig. I was relieved for that but wondered what would happen the next day when she continues to face reality. I picked up her partially eaten dinner and secured it in the kitchen.

The drama only got worse. My aunt was now officially unemployed and very miserable. The Abduls left for their homeland as planned. They gifted my aunt with some extra money, two mattresses, which we badly needed, a television set and some other household items. Still, my aunt felt the effects of not having a job anymore. She was sad too that her best friends , which was how she regarded the Abduls, would be gone from her forever. Vincent, her husband, tried to comfort her. She refused to be comforted, reminding him that he does not make much money and that my presence is an extra burden to them. All uncle Vincent said was, "Don't worry Lyn, we will make a way."

Uncle Vincent is a very kind and considerate person. His only flaw was his breath. I hate to say it but it smells like rotten eggs! I couldn't imagine how my aunt kisses him with that breath.

My aunt always did the talking and has the final say in just about every decision. Sometimes they'd be in the living room sitting down together and talking on different matters. And most times, the poor man could be seen or heard snoring away. Aunt Lyn would sometimes say to me or herself, 'he must be tired!'

Uncle Vincent was always smiling and revealing his gold mine; all of his front teeth, upper and lower, were capped in gold. According to my aunt, he migrated from Guyana with his

family when he was a teenager. They met at her cousin's wedding, became friends and were married two years later. They don't have any children since my aunt was unable to bear any, It was later discovered that my aunt had had some problems with her womb and all efforts to fix it, failed. At first, she used to say that I was her daughter but lately she seemed to feel otherwise.

Uncle Vincent works as a security guard for a private firm. He usually works the graveyard shift but occasionally he would do overtime during the day. Sometimes he'd work from eleven pm until 3pm the following day. So most times when he finally returned home after working such long hours, here goes Belinda with some other observations, the smell of his perspiration would be unbearable! And my aunt would quarrel with him sometimes, reminding him to take a good bath or else he wouldn't be sleeping in the same bed with her! But since she no longer worked, she has not said anything to him because these days she was too drunk to notice. Even uncle Vincent urged her to quit drinking.

"You going to drink yourself to death, Lyn?" he would say to his wife with great concern.

"You acting as if you lost someone," uncle Vincent continued.

Aunt Lyn sometimes in her drunkenness, would reply, "With the little money that you make, we'll never pay off our land. We can't even afford to build a proper bathroom."

Sometimes too, she would even curse him with a few expletives but as usual, he never minded.

My aunt began to blame me for everything too. One Saturday night, she was temporarily in a good mood and decided that we were going to watch TV together. I was very excited about that. I had always hoped one day that we would be blessed with such luxury as a television. It didn't seem possible but thanks to the Abdul family, we were finally blessed with such a convenience.

My aunt plugged the tv into direct current when she should have used a transformer with it. Naturally and unfortunately, the television immediately burnt out. It was the worse thing that could have even happened besides crushing my dream, my aunt who had begun drinking, blamed me for causing the damage to the television.

I explained what actually had happened to her husband but my aunt yelled over my voice;

"Don't listen to that liar. She's ruining everything around here. I'm getting fed up of that brat!"

Day by day, my aunt was becoming a monster. I lived in fear around her. I wanted to run away. But to where? I had no where to run to . My mother and younger siblings were already in St Thomas. I wished I never came to live with aunt Lyn. I initially thought it was best thing for me but it wasn't turning out that way. I really wanted to run away but I had no other family with whom to seek refuge. Uncle Arthur was no longer at the house at Brookes. And the house was being rented. When I left Brookes, I imagined it was for the better but as time moved on, I was seeing another side of aunt. She was aware of my suffering and yet she was

no longer showing compassion or care to me. I didn't realize losing the only job she ever had would turn her in such an unpleasant character.

I eventually wrote my mother and told her what was going on. She replied , suggesting that I should keep holding on for the moment.

"Hang in there Bee," my mother ended with the letter. On the contrary, it looked like aunt Lyn would hang me! All the house work still had to be done by me. Each day, my aunt would drunkenly sit and order me around. She wanted me to clean the house, mop the floor, sweep the yard and fetch water from the public pipe to fill the large water drums in the backyard. Each night, I'd go to bed drained and burdened, wishing another day would never come. But many days came and they were always the same routine. I still don't know why my aunt continue to take all of her frustrations on her niece. I now think that I must be the unluckiest person in the world, destined to suffer. Success certainly wasn't for me.

I sat down with her husband Vincent and expressed in tears what I was going through . Although he wasn't always at home, he noticed too that his wife was demanding too much from me. He too expressed disappointment in his wife and showed some signs that he too was becoming fed up with her behaviour. Who wouldn't? I thought to myself.

"People are now saying all kinds of things about my wife these days and it's embarrassing me," he shamefully disclosed.

"I really don't know why she has to take on not having a job anymore. She wasn't going to work forever!" Uncle Vincent looked puzzled.

He said he'd never imagined that his wife would one day turn out to be a drunkard. He recalled how his wife hated it whenever he took a little whisky and used to tell him that she was not sleeping with any man that drinks alcohol. Now, what is she actually doing?..... drinking more than a little, everyday. Uncle Vincent should be saying that to his wife now, the irony of it all.

I told uncle Vincent too that I am unable to go anywhere as I am always compelled to do so much in and around the house.

"She's always accusing me of doing something when I always tried my best. Yesterday, she screamed at the top of her voice, swearing to God Almighty that I stole some money from her purse. I would never do such a thing," I confidently declared.

I could see from the look on uncle Vincent's face, that he felt sorry for me. He shook his head. Eventually, he took some time off from work with the hope of helping his wife to rid her seemingly addiction to alcohol.

There was a family counsellor at the church in the village who was interested in offering her services free of charge. At first, my aunt resented the idea and claimed that she was quite okay and that her husband's imagination had run away with him. Eventually, she agreed to have the lady come to the house to speak with her. I didn't care what condition the house was in. All I wanted was some urgent intervention for my aunt.

That day when the lady came to speak with my aunt, I stayed in my bedroom and listened attentively to the session. The counsellor first prayed with my aunt and asked for God's deliverance on her soul. Then asked my aunt a series of questions and giving examples why alcohol isn't the solution to life's problems. My aunt was sometimes reluctant to reply to the counsellor's questions. When she didn't answer, her husband tried and answered the question. When the session was over, she invited my aunt and her husband to church services the following Sunday.

After the lady's first visit, there were some basic changes in my aunt's behaviour. Although she wasn't drinking like before, she still had a glass of something once in a while. Uncle Vincent got rid of all the alcohol in the house but my aunt still managed to find some elsewhere when she craved for it. There were times when my aunt would argue with her husband, plainly letting him know that she was not a child and if she was one, she certainly was not his child!

All three of us went to the church service that Sunday. It was truly a new experience for me because I had not been to a church service in a very long time. The same was for my aunt and her husband. I felt out of place among so many new faces. Everyone stared at us as if we had just landed from another planet!

I don't think we were dressed too badly though. Aunt Lyn's hairdo was a classic design. I had combed her long thick hair into four congo plaits and curled each end with roller pins. She was wearing a navy blue dress that was gifted to her by Mrs Abdul which she complimented with a pair of white dressed sandals given to her by my mother. She looked quite presentable except for that reddish lipstick plastered on her thick lips. Uncle Vincent was wearing the same black suit he'd always had and wore to every function. But the way he cared for it, one would think it was a brand new suit. I was wearing a simple white cotton dress and thought it made me looked innocent but I was extremely nervous.

Aunt Lyn suggested that we sit close to the back. The hymns were lovely and my aunt sang and clapped to some of the familiar tunes. The preacher's sermon was about the woman at the well. It touched my soul. I looked across at my aunt periodically and sensed the preacher's message touched her too. She was wiping her eyes and I felt a bit emotional.

At the end of the service, the preacher came and introduced himself to my aunt and husband. He nodded with a smile to me. Our neighbour also came to greet us.

Sister Joseph, the counsellor, made a second visit to our home and continued to lecture my aunt about the dangers of alcohol. The Sunday invitation to church service was once again offered and was taken again by us. Soon, the counsellor's visits became a routine.

Over those weeks, my aunt improved. She was not as demanding like before. She began to help me out a bit with home chores and a few times read the bible in my presence. I gradually felt much more ease around my aunt and sincerely hope that she would continue to improve.

I resumed my visits to the library. I was bored just being at home and longed to do something about my level of education. My aunt, who was no longer devilish, sometimes questioned me

rudely whenever she assumed that I might have stayed at the library too long when in fact I did return most times on time. That behaviour indicated that she had slipped back into her dinking habit.

" Belinda, where you coming from at this time?" Or, "I hope you're really coming from the library. Let me see what types of books you borrowed this time!"

"Oh Belinda, I just don't want you to meet the wrong crowd." It sounded good to hear my aunt expressed concerns for me, but I think I should be given some credit as she has seen that most of my days are spent in her casa. The only person that I usually speak with at the library is our neighbour's son, John. John is a saint and my aunt had noted many times how well- mannered he is and suggested that he was the kind of role model everyone in the village should aspire to.

The first time I spoke with John at the library, I was extremely depressed about many things, at home and in my life in general. I felt like I was heading for a real disaster because my life was insignificant and meant nothing to me. And because my aunt gave me less hope around her. I saw something in little John that I liked so I decided to confide in him that very day at the library. I was equally impressed by John's intelligence. I envisage that one day that he would become an ambassador or the leader of the country.

That same day, I had expected my aunt to be highly upset that I returned from the library an hour late than the time limit she'd given me. But surprise, surprise! She wasn't upset because she wasn't at home. There was simply a note on the dining table that read: "Your aunt is at the hospital, casualty department."

I sprinted out of the house. I was so nervous and felt my heart beating like never before. I was lucky to catch a public bus a few minutes after I raced from the house to the bus stop. Normally, it would take the bus driver twenty minutes to get to the city and would take me another ten minutes to get to the hospital by foot. But I wished I could be there in minutes.

No matter how my aunt had treated me, I wanted her to be fine. Surely, I didn't want her to die. I prayed in my mind all along that way that my aunt wasn't in a serious condition at the hospital.

My aunt had related an awful incident to me about her best friend, Rosie, who died tragically many years ago. She was only nineteen. Rosie was asthmatic. One day, they both had gone to some government office looking for a job. They were very unlucky that day. When Rosie came out of the minister's office, my aunt said that she looked very upset after she was turned down for the job. She was fretting so much that she started to breathe faster than normal. According to my aunt, Rosie collapsed on the floor in the hall of the building. She had an asthma attack. Everyone around panicked, even the lousy government minister, who all of a sudden had a change of heart when he learnt the reason why Rosie might have collapsed. But it was too late for him. Too late for all around. Rosie died on her way to the hospital.

"I was right beside her and the last words she managed to say was, "Lyn, Lyn, take this!" My aunt wiped her eyes and showed me a silver ring that Rosie gave to her seconds before she struggled to breathe in the last bit of oxygen. And seconds later, she breathed no more. My thoughts on that sad tragedy, brought back fear in my own heart, how it feels to lose someone dear to you. On my way to the hospital, my mind was falling into doubts and fear. I didn't want my aunt to blow her last breath away from this life.

When I arrived at the casualty department, I inquired about my aunt's whereabouts because she was no longer in the waiting room. A very plump nurse in white uniform immediately put on her glasses. She was moved so slowly that it must have taken her a minute to do so. She slowly looked through some papers in a folder, like she was partially blind or couldn't read at all, finally asked me in a very displeased voice, "What are you to her?"

She must have seen the panic on my face but showed no real concern. I nervously replied to her, "I'm her niece."

"I see," she said dryly. "You must wait. Her husband is the only one allowed to be with her now and he is already there with her."

"But........."

"Sorry, that's hospital rules, "the irritating nurse pointed out to me before I could say anymore.

All I wanted was to see my aunt. The inconsiderate nurse completely ignored me and my urgency. I wondered where they found people like that insensitive being. My aunt could be dying at this very minute and I just wanted to see her.

I cried and screamed so much that I drew quite a lot of attention. Eventually, another nurse came by and told me to take it easy. I tried in my weakest state, my reason for being so moved. She understood and with compassion, made a way for me to see my aunt.

She was in the observation room. I met uncle Vincent at the door. For the first time, he wasn't smiling. He looked sad and a bit tired too. I was anxious to hear any news of my aunt.

"Look," said uncle Vincent, pointing towards the left corner of the room. "There's your aunt. She's not talking. The doc said she had a stroke."

I moved closer to her bedside, crying and trembling from what I heard and saw. She was connected to lots of wires. My aunt's face was pale and at times it looked like she wasn't breathing properly.

"Is she going to die?" I foolishly asked uncle Vincent , as if like God, he would know what would be become of his wife in the end.

Uncle Vincent and I stayed until they admitted her on to a ward. The doctors told uncle Vincent that we should go home and reassured him that they would do their best to help his wife recover from the stroke. They said they'd call if they needed us urgently. Since we had no phone, we gave them our neighbour's number.

We left the hospital around half past eleven in the evening. On our way home, uncle Vincent told me what happened. He said he returned from work around two o'clock in the afternoon. He found his wife unconscious on the bed and frothing at the mouth. He said he immediately rushed to the next door neighbour and asked them to direct an ambulance to our house.

I was restless that night in bed. I turned and twisted. When I finally fell asleep, I dreamt that my aunt had died. Her spirit appeared to me and said she didn't make it to heaven. That

Satan had sent her spirit back to haunt me and her husband. She had a machete in her hand and threatened to chop my head off! I woke up screaming and soon realized that I was dreaming, thank God!

I called my mother collect, but she didn't accept the call so I tried again. She must have figured it was urgent if I insisted to call her collect, so she accepted the call. I immediately broke the news about her sister and she began 'bawling' over the phone.

"Oh Lord, oh Lord, poor sis," she screamed,

"Lord, please don't let her die. I don't even have any money to come up for the weekend to see her. Oh Lord, me belly hurting me.!"

Obviously, the way my mother was going on upset me too, so I began to cry. I told her to pray for her sister. She promised to do that and also she would send some nighties and other items.

"Say hi to my brother and sisters for me," I somehow managed to tell my mother because they were not at home.

"Okay, okay," my mom replied in a sad tone of voice,

"Please call me when you get the things I send or if anything worse happens," requested my mother before we both said goodbye and hung up the phone.

Aunt Lyn stayed quite a while in the hospital. She had some good and bad days, The folks at the church paid her several visits and prayed for her. Even our neighbour, Gwennie, helped out by offering us

meals at times. My aunt's illness brought us closer with many others. In a way, good things came from her being sick and hospitalized.

The prayers for my aunt to recover, were answered. After four weeks, three days in the hospital, unable to say a word clearly, she surprised the whole medical team in her presence by saying, 'I need a glass of water please."

Uncle Vincent and I were also in the room when it happened and we were stunned by what we heard. She recognized us and asked why she was in the hospital.

Uncle Vincent's eyes were filled with tears. He was smiling too, something I hadn't seen him done for a long time. He held on to wife's hand's hand and kissed her on the cheek saying, "All is well my dear, all is well."

It was an absolute sign that he was truly happy again. I was too.

My aunt was finally released from the hospital. The doctors were still shocked with the swift progress she made and were adamant that it couldn't be anything else but a miracle. The doctors also remarked that they never administered any major therapy to my aunt, yet she gained full

consciousness and the ability to speak and make use of both her hands without any apparent difficulty.

"Incredible," said one doctor.

When my aunt heard what had happened to her, she vowed that she was going to serve the Lord Jesus Christ as her personal saviour because He saved her for a reason. She confessed to the entire congregation one Sunday morning that if she had died on the hospital bed, she would have gone straight to hell. Many were touched by her testimony.

Total peace returned to our home. It was a huge difference. My aunt was warm and pleasant and only spoke of good. Oh, how I longed for such a day! When anyone came to visit her, she always talked about her experiences and how the Lord saved her life. She even wrote to my mother and detailed everything to her in the letter. My life was certainly getting back to normal. I no longer feared my aunt. I now know that she would not be mean to me like before.

I didn't see my neighbour John for quite a while. There were times when I went to the library and he wasn't there. We finally caught up with each other and were both happy to see each other again. He knew of my aunt's illness and recovery too.

"I have good news for you Belinda," John frantically announced.

"Really?" I asked, filled with excitement and anxious to hear the news.

"I got you enrolled in a National Development Foundation course through a friend," he further highlighted.

John told me it was a three month's course in the hospitality industry that would cover front desk, food and beverage services and housekeeping.

"Sound really good John. I would really like to take that course but I have no money to pay for it," I reluctantly added.

"Oh no Belinda, you don't have to. It's a government funded course. All one needs to do is register, which I have already done for you," John proudly declared,

My friend John deserved a hug and I gladly gave that to him. I was amazed at how a teenager like John possessed such manners, concerns for others and leadership qualities. I sometimes wished Andy was similar to him.

"Thank you so much John. You're a genius."

John handed me a piece of paper with the course information then bid me goodbye. He said he had to study for some upcoming school exam. And I sincerely wished my friend all the best.

My happy feelings and the fortunate turn of events seemed too good to be true. A new chapter has definitely turned for me and its contents seemed to be pointed in the right direction.

The new aunt Lyn was elated for me and my ambitions.

"God made a way for you my dear," she said to me calmly and positively. She also confessed that was too hard on me and she now realized how much she was hurting me inside.

"The devil was really controlling my life," she said.

"Bee, you expected me to be an example. I know you expected me to be different and that's why I brought you from Brookes.

I had problems of my own and didn't deal with them the right way so I took it out on you at times and on my husband other times. Thank God for having come to my rescue. I am new creature in Christ now."

She embraced me tenderly like I was something fragile that she did not want to break. No doubt she meant every word. Honestly, I couldn't wait for the days ahead of me. I was anxious, especially to find out how I would adapt to my new adventures.

My aunt must have read my mind, as she was still embracing me, she said in such a nice, whispering voice:

"Bee, everything will be fine, everything will be fine. Just trust in the Lord."

I searched for a piece of blank paper and a writing tool. When I was successful, I scribbled on the paper a proverb I learnt at school; "Good things come to those who wait."

OF BLESSINGS AND
OF CHALLENGES

Twenty-four students were enrolled in the hospitality industry course. It was held at the government primary school in the village every Monday to Friday from seven o'clock in the evening, exactly for two hours. Mrs Cynthia Wilkins was the lecturer. She was very serious about what she taught and many of my classmates referred to as Mrs Strictland, behind her back, of course!

On the first day of class, everyone had to make a personal introduction. I was nervous and felt like it was my very first day at primary school. A little bit of my nervousness was taken away when I received a thunderous applause from the class after I made my personal introduction.

"Okay class, thank you all for your individual introductions. Now, it's my turn and I would like that all of you listen to me attentively, Mrs Wilkins warmly announced. According to her, she has been working within the tourism industry for over thirteen years. She graduated from Cornell University in the United States with a master's degree in Tourism and Hospitality Management with French. She announced too that her husband has also been working within the same sector for over eighteen years. They have only one child, a daughter who was currently studying Law in England.

"I expect all of you to attend classes and also to be punctual at all times. If you are unable to make it for class, please let me know in advance, Mrs Wilkins emphasized.

"You must be serious about the course as it is important to learn more about our main industry, tourism. And how we can all make a difference or contribution to that industry by becoming more knowledgeable and subsequently, skilled."

Mrs Wilkins went on and on about what she expected from us during the course. She stressed that our overall performance would be graded and rated, thus giving us the opportunity to be placed within the workforce, usually at selected hotels or restaurants at the end of the course.

I knew this course was an opportunity for me to enter the workforce for the first time. Therefore, it was essential for me to complete the course by studying hard and succeed in the end. Then, I would be so proud of myself.

Mrs Wilkins handed each of us a booklet that outlined the subjects and lessons that would be covered during the course. Everyone seemed very interested. When she was finished, she

opened the floor to anyone who wished to ask any relevant questions. The response was great and in the end, we all promised to do our best during the three month course.

I was very surprised to receive a letter from my eldest brother, Andy. I didn't even know that he had actually left the island. He stated in the letter that he was now living in Switzerland with his wife, Anne. He went on to say that his wife would be giving birth to their first child at the end of November. When I really thought about it, it matches in character for Andy to end up doing something like that. He was always around white women. I hoped that he didn't marry one old enough to be his mother! Anyway, if he actually did, that would be his choice and his business. Afterall, my brother is an adult.

My brother did not send me any photos but promised to do so in his next letter to me. He also requested that I provide him with our mother's address and telephone number. He and his wife were planning to visit her on their next holiday, sometime next year. Andy also enclosed a cheque worth just over one hundred American dollars written to me. He really surprised me with that. He must have married a filthy rich woman or he has a good paying job. I was very happy and grateful for the money because I was tired of leaning on my aunt and her husband for just about everything. So the cheque could not have arrived at a better time.

I was really elated to hear from Andy. He also said sorry for having previously isolated himself from the family and could never blame me for what had transpired in his life then. He had no idea what I had been through. Most importantly, he wanted us to reconnect and that for sure would happen, no doubt.

Classes have been going on quite well. We were already in the third week of the course. However, one Wednesday evening, something dramatic happened in the class. Mrs

Wilkins assigned some class work for us while she went on an urgent errand. She didn't anticipate that there would be any problem because we aren't a bunch of kids. However, two female students got into some quarrel which resulted in a fight. When the fight ended, one got a busted lip and the other a small cut over her right eye. Apparently, the two women were fighting for some man they both were in love or in lust with named Alfred. It was later rumoured that Alfred was the husband of one of the women involved in the fracas.

All kind of stories were jumping out some of the classmates mouths like jumping jacks. Alfred's wife, Loretta, was accusing Janice of having an affair with her husband. Scandalous!

Even though the fight was over, complete order was still lacking. Both young women were now at either end of the classroom, each held by someone, continued to exchange bitter words with each other.

"Janice, if you don't stop sleeping with my husband, you'll see what I'll do to you," shouted Loretta in such a rage as she tried hard to free herself from Dion's grip. She wanted to fight Janice again.

Janice with her busted and swollen lips, looked a bit ashamed and simply replied:

"I am going to get my lawyer after you if you don't stop scandalizing my name."

No sooner had Janice finished saying those words Loretta quickly fired back. She reminded Janice she was the one who would have the law on her side because Janice was trying to break up her marriage.

My classmates and I continued to appease the two women when Mrs Wilkins returned. She expressed her profound disappointment over the incident and openly told the two young women that she couldn't afford for them to continue the course.

"How could one expect to work in the hospitality industry and exhibit such distasteful conduct? That's unbecoming of the ideal candidates," Mrs Wilkins pointed out to us in such a forceful manner that gave us enough reasons to realize that under no circumstances she would tolerate any students who conducted themselves in such a manner like Loretta and Janice did. In all fairness, she was right.

After class, many of the students congregated outside to discuss what had happened between Janice and Loretta. Some made fun of Janice, suggesting that she should learn to leave other people's property alone. She was also blamed for being too blatant with her lifestyle. It was rumoured that she had been dating older men, especially married ones, since she was fifteen. I was also mortified to learn that her mother was running after younger men. No wonder she had not objected to her daughter's lifestyle. Others showed pity on Loretta. Personally, Loretta was doing quite well in class and I am confident that if she was allowed to continue the course, she would have been successful in the end. Although I never showed it openly, I didn't like Janice that much. She was always pushing herself pridefully in front of everybody and sadly she reaped only one thing today, a fall. It serves her right.

Loretta and I became good friends. She was the only girlfriend that I ever had. She told me about the problems she has been having with her husband recently.

One of the girls saw Janice and my husband at the cinema recently," Loretta mentioned to me the last time we went to the library, Loretta eventually spoke to her husband about it and he flatly denied it saying that he hardly knew the woman. He said that she had only come into his office a few times to deal with a criminal matter. Loretta's husband is a policeman and works at the criminal investigation department at the police headquarters in the city. They have a nine -month old baby boy named after his father. Loretta concluded that she was still suspicious of him and would be monitoring the situation closely.

Rumour had it too that Loretta was told by another classmate Brenda, that she saw Janice with a picture of her husband. When Loretta confronted Janice, an argument ensued between the two. It was unfortunate that it ended up the way it did, especially for Loretta.

One would conclude that Loretta must have really been fed up with all the rumours she was hearing about her husband and Janice and lost it that day. I personally share that sentiment too.

I met up with John the following week at a social gathering, organised by the church we both go to, although I should confess that John frequents the church more than I do.

"Nice to see you, John," I greeted him with my usual smile. He was standing with a group of young people to whom he introduced me. I noticed there was young lady who was always

standing at his side. Later, in our conversation, John disclosed to me that the young lady is in fact his girlfriend. They met at some inter-school science show. I was dying to tease him about his new luck and the moment his girlfriend left for the bathroom, we both laughed simultaneously.

"Now Belinda, isn't she beautiful?" John beamed and proudly asked. He looked desperate to hear my response.

"Oh John, she's beautiful and I am so happy for you," I excitedly replied.

"I am almost over the rainbow, and not the moon, since I found Charmaine," remarked John frantically.

I was truly happy for him. I sensed that he and Charmaine are smart enough to maintain a decent relationship, unlike many of the other young folks who make disasters of their so called relationships.

By the time Charmaine returned, John had already filled me in on some details about her. She's attending the Faith Girls High School, where she's been nominated head girl for two consecutive years. Besides being an 'A' student, she is already fluent in both French and Spanish. She hopes one day to become a professor of languages, primarily to teach English, French and Spanish. She and John would graduate from high school next year. Charmaine would be going off to England to further her studies. Her father lives there and apparently had already begun making preparations for his daughter's arrival. John also told me he has an uncle in England, who would like to see him go on to tertiary education. His uncle, according to his nephew, promised to assist him financially with that. John expressed his delight about his uncle's interest in his education and naturally welcomed the offer. His goal is to pursue his tertiary education in England so that he would be not too far from his girlfriend.

While I commended John and Charmaine on their dedication to their education, I began to reflect on what might have been or could have been , had I completed high school. I wasn't jealous of my friends' achievements, but I know that I was also capable of excelling in my studies, had I been given the opportunity. I reflected further too, that even I completed high school and did well, I still would not have been able to pursue higher education at home or abroad. I am not as fortunate as John and Charmaine. I couldn't think of anyone in my family who would be able to afford the costs involved. I was satisfied that what was going within my mind didn't reflect on the outside, while I conversed with John and Charmaine.

Let me create this scenario. Belinda is a top student. Among the best three students in her class. Excellent at the sciences. And one day, she promised that she would really make her grandma proud. Belinda becomes a lawyer and doing well. All this is pure imagination and wishful thinking because I cannot turn dreams into reality without actual help. And such 'what could be, would be' reflection made my heart so weak. So very weak.

With a heavy head and many memories and wishes, I laid on my bed. I heard my grandmother's voice whispering gently in my ears how she was so proud of me and that one day I was going to make her, myself and my family proud too. I remembered that day when I was in school and the teacher read out loud the first poem I had ever written. She remarked what a creative mind I possessed and congratulated me. I remembered her going over and over the first verse of my poem, reading it with such a meaning that I was convinced in the end that my poem had an effect on her.

Hold on to the truth as you can,

try not to lie to anyone,

think highly of yourself, you'll see,

You'll understand................

why life sometimes isn't easy.

The words of my poem returned to me so clearly. I felt somewhat emotional. I sobbed as much as I wanted to. Life truly had not been easy for me. I talked to God asked Him many questions. I wasn't sure He heard me. I felt so negative in that moment. I felt I was a born loser. All I could hear in my mind, 'It's too late Belinda. You won't make it, no matter how hard you try.'

Aunt Lyn's younger brother, Arthur, turned up for a visit, something he hadn't done in a very long time. She was happy to see him. They hugged each other for a long time , like it was going out of style!

"Oh bro, what has become of you? You look so different" My aunt was right. Uncle Arthur looked like an old man. He had a forest of beard. And his hair on his head looked like he hasn't combed it for ages.

"Sis, it's all that hard work I do for that woman of mine. She causes me too much headache too because of her jealousy," uncle Arthur revealed to his sister.

"But Arthur, you never brought your woman here to introduce her to me," my aunt noted to her brother.

"It's the time sis, just time. Always told myself I would bring my kids and my girlfriend to see you, but I never got the chance," explained her brother, but in a tone that suggested he was troubled over something or someone.

From my own observation, uncle Arthur seemed weighed down by many problems. They must have been so overpowering now that he finally came to see his sister.

"My brother, I am now a christian. The Lord saved me from death's bed and I promised that I would serve Him for as long as I live," declared aunt Lyn in such a proud manner. She continued: " I have asked the Lord to bring you to me because I have been concerned about everyone of you. I thought why you were not coming to see your sister."

Uncle Arthur revealed to his sister what was bothering him. By the time he finished relating his story, his sister knew who he was talking about. And it was for the first time since my aunt claimed christianity, that I witnessed such a wicked look on her face. It expressed total disappointment and scorn.

"Arthur, how could you have ever thought of having a relationship with that woman when you knew what she did to us?" questioned my aunt.

At that point, she was standing, akimbo in front of her brother, who was seated on a chair. My aunt sounded devilish, like she had for that moment, completely forgot that she had given her life to Christ.

"Sis, sis, I, I don't know how it ha-happened but I like her very much," uncle Arthur slightly stammered with his answer sealed with a confession.

Aunt Lyn solidly slapped her brother across his face, the moment he uttered , 'I like her very much.' I was shocked and convinced that the devil had definitely gotten into my aunt. She was still standing in front of her brother, shaking like a leaf!

She asked her brother if he remembered the troubles Bernita and her mother caused the family many years ago. My aunt reminded her brother of the incidents which obviously were still fresh on her mind.

"First, it was Bernita's mother, Jane-Anne, who tried many times to break up our parent's marriage. She even told the world that one of her daughters belonged to papa, how dare her?" recalled my aunt, slightly fuming and a hint of teary eyes.

Aunt Lyn continued to lecture her brother why Bernita was not the one with whom he should have had a relationship much less being the father of her kids.

My aunt also accused Bernita and her mother of verbally abusing my dear grandma on numerous occasions. Bernita was also alleged to have hit my grandmother on her shoulder with a skipping rope rod during one of their confrontations. I had already been fuming having heard what my aunt was relating about this Bernita person and her mother. But having just heard that she was alleged to have hit my grandmother, made me ever more upset. Uncle Arthur noticed the fury on my face. He could not afford to say anything. He just continued to bow his head as if looking forward or upward was too much for him. Too bad. He should have known better and never even thought of being a mutual friend with that Bernita.

When he became involved with Bernita, he knew that not a soul in the family would be pleased. I now could see aunt Lyn's reason for being so upset. Besides, from what I have heard, my uncle was much younger than Bernita.

It was a well known fact in the community that my grandparents did not like trouble. They welcomed peace any day instead. Despite all of Bernita's and her mother's malicious acts, my grandparents never bothered to take them to court. Instead, they took them to the Lord in prayers. It was said that Bernita's mother was cut off from this life without remedy. Apparently, Bernita had to throw 'some dry corn' down her mother's throat while she was dying, to stop her from confessing to all of the bad deeds she had done to many people in her younger years. Everyone one of her children were obviously embarrassed over the situation.

Aunt Lyn sated loud and clear to her brother that Bernita would always make him unhappy citing she has a mind of her own.

"Mark you, look after the twins, if they are really yours!" exclaimed my aunt, still standing in front of her brother.

"And forget about any wedding with that vile creature. That woman only wants to show the world that she has a ring on her finger and that's all there is to it," warned my aunt.

My aunt begged her brother to think more on the Lord and allow Him to lead in the right direction. Before uncle Arthur left, his sister prayed with him and further encouraged him to give his life to Christ. In her prayers, she also asked for forgiveness knowing that she did not act christian-like during most of the discussions she had with her brother.

Uncle Arthur definitely left with a different and perhaps a better mood than what he came with. Personally speaking, he would be better off forgetting that Bernita and take care of the twins, if they are really his, a sentiment I also shared with my aunt. And move on with his life. Of course, that is easier said than done. It is very difficult for my family to think uncle Arthur would think that staying with Bernita would be the best thing that ever happened to him. It is sad to think about that uncle Arthur might in truth, had already thought that Bernita is the right woman for him.

It had been a while since I last spoke with my mother. Most of the times when I called her collect, my younger siblings were not at home. According to mother, they spend a lot of time doing extracurricular activities or doing something with their neighbour's children.

"So how's my daughter doing," mother asked sounding quite cheerful. I told her that I was doing okay and so were her sister and husband. Of course, I also mentioned the latest about uncle Arthur and Bernita. There was an immediate silence on the line. After a few seconds, I had to ask my mother if she was still there.

"You're kidding me, Bee. My brother's head must be cooked. How could he ever think of having a relationship with that old fart!" screamed my mother over the phone.

The way mother expressed herself over the phone, even a fool would know she was angry. She lamented over and over again that none of her brothers had any class or taste, except in their gender and taste buds.

I wasn't going to say anything about that. When mother finally had her say about her brother and Bernita, she switched to another subject, like a sudden awakening. She talked about my brother and sisters and boasted how very well they were doing in school. Although I didn't

let it show in my voice, I was again rather disappointed that I didn't get a chance to chitchat with them too.

Before we hung up the phone, mother said that she had written me a letter in which she enclosed some recent photos of herself and my siblings. I was happy to hear that news since it indicated that mother did receive my correspondence. I was looking forward to see to those photos and wished the postman would arrive with the letter tomorrow!

Before I started the hospitality industry course, I promised myself that I would never miss a class, no matter what. I don't want to break that promise. The rains were pouring down in buckets and non- stop for the last forty minutes or so , with no sign that it was going to end soon. I was still very determined to get to class. My aunt even discouraged me not to go.

"Cant you see the weather is bad Bee?" My aunt reminded me, a few times within a few minutes.

In the end, I didn't listen to her. When the rain subsided a bit, I took my bag and was on my way out of the house.

Quite a few people didn't show up for class but Mrs Wilkins, who wouldn't miss lecturing for the world, suggested that class must go on with or 'sans' everybody. During class, I noticed one of the guys, Alvin, kept smartly staring at me. I deliberately looked the other way for a brief moment then returned my eyes to his direction. And each time, I caught him still staring at me. When Mrs Wilkins dismissed class, I felt a bit relieved. Alvin's staring had me somewhat nervous. It was not the first time that I caught him staring at me but it was not so intense previously. He is a handsome chap, with full brown eyes.

"Belinda, can I say something to you?" Alvin stammered. He sounded nervous too. I was about to exit the school gate when he approached me. He told me that he has been thinking about me for a long time. At first, I didn't know what to say to him so I just hastily replied:

"Alvin, I'm sorry but maybe we could chat more another time." I showed no signs of nervousness that time but deep inside me, I was nervous as hell.

"Please Belinda, it's not too late. The weather is much better now. Let's go somewhere privately and talk for a bit," Alvin, calmly and politely suggested.

I was still hesitant. In fact, I wasn't ready to talk to any guy yet. I sensed Alvin's urgency to have a broader chat with me. I didn't feel ready to start a relationship with a man.

But Alvin continued to beg me not to return home without chatting further with him. So surprise, surprise, I finally decided to give him a listening ear.

"Okay, you win Alvin," I declared.

Grinning from ear to ear and looking as if he's been just told that he won a million dollars, Alvin couldn't stop thanking me for agreeing to his request. All kinds of thoughts were rushing through my head. Those horrible incidents with my horrible uncle Jim came from my subconscious mind to haunt me. Thinking about that, the look on my face suddenly changed. Alvin, noticed that I wasn't saying much, looked at me shyly and asked if I was okay. My response to him was that I was feeling a bit timid.

We had walked to the school's playground. It was nicely lit with floodlights. That made me felt more comfortable. No one was in sight, except for the security guard, who came by and questioned us. He looked satisfied and reminded us to lock the school gate when were leaving.

Alvin wanted a girlfriend. He didn't waste anytime bringing out that magic word. According to him, he had a two year relationship with some girl from the city but said she left in March earlier this year for New York. From the information he's shared with me, it was obvious that her departure has left some void in his love life.

"She really meant a lot to me," Alvin noted, looking distant. He thought that the relationship would continue, even though she was abroad, but it didn't. Despite having visited her a few times, Alvin said he received a letter from her, telling him that she wanted to move on with her life. He also cited that her reason was because they were now living too far apart from each other. Laurie-Anne concluded that she would always love Alvin but preferred that they remain being just platonic friends. He said he was still baffled at Laurie Anne's drastic decision and admitted that he was still hurt over it.

Even an inexperienced person like me could figure out what Alvin's ex was up to. Maybe he could too but was not ready to face the reality of it. The way I saw it, Alvin's ex was seeing another man and she doesn't want to break Alvin's heart, so she tried to play smart by not revealing the real reason behind her decision.

When Alvin told me that he fancies me a lot, I immediately asked him what he saw in me.

"You have a beautiful smile and I am just in love with you," he quickly replied with all smiles.

I didn't know I was blushing until he drew my attention to the fact. I told Alvin that I would think about the offer. I needed time to reflect and to think about having an actual relationship with a guy. It wasn't like taking a pen and a piece of paper and write what comes to mind in that moment. It was about a relationship between two people. Admittedly, Alvin is one handsome fella but I just couldn't give in to a man's request for a relationship so easily and

certainly not in one night! Besides, what if the story of what he related to me about Laurie-Anne was not true? I did accept his invitation to take me to the movies though.

That night we both left with a lot on our minds. Alvin wanted to call me when he got home but was very disappointed to learn that we didn't have a telephone at home. He promised that he was going to try his best to get us a landline as soon as possible. He was working part-time at the National Telephone Company, N-Tel.

When I returned home that night, my aunt and her husband were up watching television. That wasn't something unusual but as soon as I closed the front door behind me and walked through the living room, I realized that my aunt was staring at me, more than she had done in recent times. Instantly, I figured out she want to ask me where I had been.

"Bee, I thought something happened to you. Why are you coming back so late from class? my aunt interrogated.

I wasn't ready to tell her anything about Alvin since I would need time myself to figure that out. I lied and told my aunt that one of the girls at school invited me for dinner at her house for her birthday. My aunt understood and posed no further questions. As for me, there was nothing to celebrate. I was hungry but I couldn't eat the dinner that had been left for me without arousing my aunt's suspicions. My aunt knows that I generally don't each much. Truly, I eat like a bird. Uncle Vincent was the quite the opposite. He eats like a horse! That's why I wasn't surprised when he said to his wife that he would eat the dinner that was left for me before he goes to bed.

My aunt had cooked something I love, smoked herring, chopped spinach and softly boiled white dumplings. The thought of not having it, made my stomach craved more for it. I wished

I didn't lie to my aunt. I should have thought of another excuse, rather than that old silly story about some friend's birthday party that never happened. The price one pays for lying, can be a pain in one's stomach as it was in my case, this very minute.

I resorted to a glass of cold, locally made ginger beer and headed for my bedroom. I had no intentions of going to sleep right away. There was too much to think about, especially Alvin's proposal. I had never given any thought or serious consideration of finding a man or a man finding me, whichever sounded better! I had read many romance novels about men and women who fell in and out of love. I used to get caught up with the stories that I decided that I wouldn't read them anymore. Alvin wanted to have a relationship with me, but I was concerned about his intentions too. I didn't want a man to be only interested in my body. I didn't think Alvin would be that type of guy but you can't know something like that about a man after only one night of very deep conversations.

"Take him girl! Now is your time," my imaginative voice yelled from within me. I wanted to, but I was afraid I would eventually have to explain to Alvin why I was no longer a virgin should we become lovers and possibly get intimate or even get married ! There, the bastard,

my so called uncle Jim, came into the picture again. I was fuming with so much dislike for him. How could he have been so uncaring , so evil , to have used his niece as his sexual slave. At fifteen, my sick uncle sexually molested me over and over again. And each time he satisfied his dirty desire, he had the nerve to look at his helpless niece and remarked:

"I know you like it now. It's not too big for you anymore..."

Can you imagine how that made me feel? And now he is making everything look so bad on my life and on my own behalf, thanks Jimmy boy. Thanks for your tar on my life!

"So what," I thought to myself. I am not the only girl in the world who was sexually molested by a relative. I know that the scar won't go away but live goes on. I don't intend to live always without a man in my life. Maybe he can heal some of my wounds while still adding some spice to my life.

So, in the end, after much thoughts and deliberations, I decided to say yes to Alvin's relationship proposal. But, I would be in no hurry to go to bed with him, if that was all he was after. Even being naïve about relationships, I am aware that giving my all to a man too early, would only give him an excuse to dump me for no reason.

Thinking about Alvin left me exhausted and sleepy. In a short time, I was in dreamland, dreaming about him! In my dream, Alvin had asked me to accompany him to his home to pick up of some textbooks that he had forgotten to take to class. When we got there, he invited me to his bedroom. I sat on his bedside and sooner I had done so, Alvin was sitting next to me. Without warning, he caressed me and kissed me tenderly around my neck and on my cheeks. After only a few minutes, we were both lying naked in his bed. He then mounted me. His penis was so s short that the insertion was easy. However, he pounded me like a

jackhammer and I was enjoying the moment. We both simultaneously arrived at our destination. Alvin was tired but I wasn't. I wanted more but Alvin's littleness was too flaccid to continue. I was so disappointed so I began to curse him and told him he couldn't satisfy a bitch like me!

I suddenly awoke, realizing it had all been a dream, but I felt totally ashamed, nonetheless. Ashamed how vulgar and freely my thoughts were captured in that dream.

When I told Alvin that I would like to have a relationship with him, he literally lifted me in his arms like I was an overgrown baby. I was slightly embarrassed because it happened on the streets, in public view. We had just walked a few yards from the cinema when I broke the news.

"Oh, Alvin, you can put me down now," I said, sounding a bit joyful but reluctant. He did as I requested and replied in a soft masculine voice that made my heart danced with happiness.

"Anything for you, darling."

Our relationship started off in good faith. Alvin's presence in my life was dawning to mean a lot to me, each passing day. I never felt loved like that before. Considering all the ups and downs in my life, I felt that the moment has arrived and somehow, Alvin at twenty , possessed so much real love , maturity and understanding. We were looking more like a couple as time passed by. Even though Alvin was anxious to go further than simply dating, I reminded him that we both needed to give ourselves more time before rushing into the deeper intimacy of our relationship. He showed understanding but deep down, I sensed he wanted us to do more than just meeting for lunch, dinner, drinks, walks and the movies. But he also wanted to make me feel comfortable around him. Since Alvin got the telephone installed at my aunt's home, he never failed to telephone me when he said he was going to.

My aunt remarked too that he seemed to be a nice guy and encouraged both of us to give our hearts to the Lord and He certainly would direct our paths.

Everyone began to notice a sparkle in me. Some ladies who attend the hospitality course, were already calling me Mrs Lindsay. Alvin liked to hear that and sometimes would reply to the ladies, smiling all the way, "Are you jealous or what?" Whether or not he meant it , he was smiling effortlessly when he said it. Even John, my neighbour, was on my case.

He said to me one day: "So we are in the same boat now, aren't we Belinda?" I just laughed at him and told him to give me a break!

Alvin and I did many things together. He took me out for lunch and dinner. He also took me fishing with his friends, around the island boat cruises , concerts, just about anything to make me happy. Sometimes, we'd study together and we both would do well on our exams. I questioned him about his interest in the course when he already had his hands full with job at N-Tel. He expressed his passion for food and beverage and mentioned that he wouldn't mind becoming a part-time bartender on evening shifts. Andy said too that he has big plans for the future and realized that the extra money that he could earn from bartendering, would bring him closer to his plan. According to him, he had already purchased a piece of prime residential land on the north of the island with the intention to build his dream house on it. And my young man also has hopes of marrying by the time he turns twenty -four and to father two children eventually and hopefully a boy and a girl, unless the Lord decides otherwise. I am so impressed with Alvin, at such a young age, he has accomplished some major milestones in his life and he is not the typical young man with all of his ambitions.

Mother called one night to say that she'd heard I finally found a boyfriend and that she only called to congratulate me and that I should be careful. I was rather surprised to hear from her with that revelation. Her sister must have phoned her with the news about Alvin and I. As we spoke, I could hear my siblings in the background. I was finally able to speak with my darling siblings who all shared their great achievements in school. I congratulated them and thanked for the lovely photos I received of them.

"Our mother said that we might come up there for summer sis," Samantha excitedly announced. I could hear the excitement of the others in the background at the news of the trip.

"That would be so nice, Sammie," I responded enthusiastically.

"Okay, Sammie, that's enough talking now. Say bye to your sister," mother politely advised Samantha.

"Take care Sammie, and kiss the others for me," I softly requested.

Mother came back on the line to tell me she written another letter, telling us about possibility that the kids would be coming for summer vacation.

"It all depends Bee. Money isn't too plentiful but we will see."

"Then let's not run up the bill any higher mother. Did you want me to tell your sister you called?"

"That's alright dear. I spoke with her yesterday," she replied.

"Well then, see you mom and have a good night."

"See you too dear and take care of yourself," reminded mother before we hung up the phone from each other.

No sooner than the cradle of the phone was firmly placed in its position than it rang again. It was Alvin. He wanted to know why the telephone line was busy for so long.

"I was talking to my mother and siblings in St Thomas," I informed my inquisitive boyfriend.

He sounded relieved. I had completely forgotten that Alvin and I had planned to study

together at his home. I honestly wasn't in the mood so I disappointed him by letting him know that I wasn't feeling too well and would rather stay at home. He also realized it was that time of the month, so he forgave me.

We didn't get off the phone right away. In fact, we talked and talked as if there wouldn't be a bill at the end of the month. When Alvin felt satisfied that he had given me enough comforting words for the night, he blew kisses over the phone and whispered in his sexiest voice yet;

"Feel the warmth of my sweet lips on yours, my darling. And when you go to bed , dream of me." Once more,

Alvin knocked me over figuratively with his powerful voice. Although I wanted to get on with my studies before I went to bed ,I shamelessly felt aroused. He was no longer on the line and I didn't want to call him again. I continued to reserve myself for the big day when we would go beyond kissing . Thinking about it, heightened my passion , so I decided to take a cold bath.

It was about two in the morning when I decided that I had enough of studying for one night. We were going to have final exams in a few weeks and graduation would follow shortly after that. Mrs Wilkins had told us that three professionals from the tourist trade, would be coming to our classes during the coming week. They would be evaluating how well we have applied ourselves during the course. I certainly didn't want to come so far and only end up failing in the end. If that were to happen, I would be devastated. I kept thinking how nice it would be to start a job and earn my own money. I didn't care if I would not be earning much money in the beginning. Just to experience working in the real world, would mean a lot to me.

I thank God, my dear brother Andy, who many thought would not make it in life. He was the one responsible for supporting me financially from time to time. He has promised also to cover all expenses for my graduation, further cementing my gratitude to him, forever.

I was relieved when final exams were over. I had done my best and anticipated positive results. When the results were released, I was placed among the top five students. Because of that, I was guaranteed a place in the program, with an option to choose an establishment where I would like to work. We were already given a list of all the hotels and restaurants affiliated with the program and their order of rating. Alvin was not among the top five students, but he did pass his course and also earned a place of his choice. We were both happy for each other.

The wonderful boy who made part of my dream possible, had the right to know about my success. I paid him a visit and he was delighted to see me.

"Belinda, I knew you would do well," John exclaimed with pure excitement.

"And John, my friend, it all started with you. You made this moment possible. And come what may, I promise to get you something nice from my first earnings."

He smiled and responded, "You don't have to, Belinda. I'm just so very pleased for you and your achievements."

"But you know I would do it anyway," I softly but firmly replied.

His mother was there too. She also expressed her happiness at my success and wished me all the best. I gave them both an invitation to our commencement exercises. John assured me that he wouldn't miss for the world!

The big day came. The stage was set. Mrs Wilkins welcomed the audience. The minister of tourism gave the commencement address. He was boring and I breathed a sigh of relief when he finally finished, even I applauded louder for him than anyone else in the audience. A representative from the Hotel and Tourist Association , presented us with medals and certificates.

The main highlight of the ceremony, was a special presentation by all of the graduates, themed, "On our Way." It was well put together and the audience was thrilled by it. I glimpsed my aunt and her husband in the audience, looking proud and happy for me. I also saw

John, his girlfriend and his mother. They all came to support me, which made me felt very special.

The graduation ball was held at Octagon Palace, located on the famous Broad Lane Avenue in the heart of the city. We doffed our graduation gowns and were left in our very best attires, which we all planned for the ball. Alvin had already promised that we'd be dancing the night away. And that we definitely did! I had never been to a dance before and apparently, I surprised everyone with my dance moves, including Alvin. I did practice a lot before that night I should confess. The way Alvin and I moved on the dance floor, gave onlookers the impression that we have been dancing together for years. Almost everyone was paired off on the dance floor. Even Mrs Wilkins. She wasn't a great dancer, but she appeared to be having a good time. She had worked very hard, so she deserved a night to let loose!

By the end of the dance, I had consumed four glasses of champagne. Alvin had more and smelled like a rum bottle! He had already asked me to spend the night at his place. The night has been going on fantastically well that I didn't want it to end. I was in euphoria. And having had that much of champagne, it was so easy for me to think that spending the night at

Alvin's , would make the day complete. I didn't want to be an angel in Alvin's eyes anymore.

I finally gave in to Alvin. I was very much surprised by his charisma, even though it was evident that both us were under the influence of alcohol. But my faculty was still in place. And experiencing Alvin in person , was unlike that dream I had about him. My boyfriend was well endowed too! I wasn't even aware before that I was able to consume different types of alcohol and still had good memory. I requested a glass of wine. My dear heart satisfied me and I didn't regret my decision to sleep with him.

I started working as a receptionist at the Oceania Resort as a receptionist, two weeks after graduation. It definitely was a brand new experience for me and I loved every minute of it. Mother sent me two pairs of working shoes and some toiletries. The resort gave me a pair of uniform, so I didn't have to worry about getting a new wardrobe right away. Meanwhile, my boyfriend was lucky to find another part time job, working in the evenings at the Palm Tree Restaurant as a bartender.

Oceania Resort is among the top fifty five star resorts of the world. Owned by a group of local, regional and European investors, the resort boasts of having some of the finest amenities available in the trade for its guests. But it costs an arm and a leg and possibly more to spend just one night at the resort. Many famous people are known to frequent the resort and just recently, during my first week there, I met my favourite country and western singer. He was a disappointment though. I wondered who he trying to impress by walking around in

his swimsuit with an artificial bulge. A good source revealed that she, apparently had all of it at one go in her mouth!

Alvin and I still found time for each other. He was working four nights a week while I was working five days, with a mixture of morning and afternoon shifts.

When I received my first wages, I felt like I had just received a million dollars. A million dollars that couldn't buy much but I was content and felt independent. I bought John a scientific calculator. I made certain that I kept my word. Though it wasn't the greatest of gifts, it came from my heart. John knew that it was genuinely given and he thanked me very much for the gift.

Alvin and I continued spending time together, whenever we can, until one day he told me he was going to travel to New York for a couple of days. Truthfully, I was quite surprised since he never gave me any previous indication that he had planned to travel. I suspected that his ex girlfriend was the main reason for his trip but I didn't say anything to him. Before he left, he begged me not to worry about him or anything, assuring me that he still loved me and would never do anything to hurt me. I believed him to a certain extent but in the back of my mind, I sensed that he was going to New York to see Laurie-Anne. I couldn't accuse Alvin because I had no evidence that he was still in touch with Laurie-Anne. Only some months ago, I discovered a passport sized picture of a young lady that fell from his wallet and he said it was Laurie-Anne. I demanded that he got rid of it, which he did in my presence.

I later discovered that Laurie-Anne had returned to the island on the same flight with Alvin. I had a fit over it and developed an enormous headache instantly. When I confronted him, he told me it was just coincidental. He swore that he and Laurie-Anne were no longer friends and stressed that he was still in love with me and nobody else.

As time went by, the evidence against his words, gradually unfolded. Alvin would call to say that he was coming over, but he never came. His lovemaking became sloppy. He was always in a hurry to leave whenever we went out. I soon became very convinced that Alvin was involved with someone else, if not Laurie-Anne. I was determined to find out what my 'now question mark boyfriend' was really up to these days. He has to be proven innocent or guilty, one way or the other.

One Sunday even, after Alvin and I went to the cinema, I pretended that I was tired and begged him to take me home. He didn't hesitate to do so. But I was far from being tired. I was up to something. After waited long enough and judged that the was definitely at home then, I took a taxi to his house and quietly entered the house with the keys he'd given to me. His bedroom soft red lights were on. From my own experience there, that only happened when we were spending a romantic time. I was anxious to know what was really happening within that bedroom and I wasn't even there. Our favourite music was playing and my heart was beating abnormally. I took a deep breath and quietly turned the knob on his bedroom door. It wasn't locked so opened it and found Alvin and another woman moaning and kissing passionately.

"I can see you Alvin!" I announced in a teary voice. Alvin was shocked to see me. The guilt registered on his face. He was covering his private parts as if he was covering up his nakedness from a total stranger. He drowned me with disbelief.

When the young woman looked at me, bewildered, too, I knew it was Laurie -Anne. I couldn't believe my eyes. I trusted Alvin so much and thought we had a good relationship. Now the evidence bears before me that he was definitely lying to me.

I didn't want to hear his explanation. I left, completely devastated. I returned home in a rush. I cried for my drowning relationship.

I tried hard not to let Alvin's betrayal jeopardized my performances at work. Slowly, day by day, I learned to deal with my heartbreak. Alvin had the audacity to call me several times and even came by to see me but I was too hurt and felt betrayed to even continue any relationship with him. Deep inside my heart, I missed him and needed him badly but I fought back hard and was learning to live without him. He was the first love of my life so it hurts to carry on life without him, even though I witnessed he cheated on me.

It was weeks after the incident I told my mother and aunt about Alvin. I didn't go into details though. I only told them that he was back with his ex.

"Maybe he wasn't for you , dear," my aunt hinted as she tried to comfort me.

Mother suggested that I forget about him and to move on with my life.

"Bee, you're pretty and thoughtful young lady, sooner or later, a nice gentleman will come your way," my mother further informed. She sounded hopeful for me.

Since I broke up with Alvin, I promised myself that I wouldn't be in any hurry to find another boyfriend, I didn't want to be hurt like that again. I concluded too that all men are the same. I didn't want to think about falling in love again, but apparently, I was getting over Alvin, much sooner than I thought!

I eventually met a wonderful man at a nightclub where sometimes, me and a few girls from the front desk hang out. However, I decided not to rush into anything soon as recent experience has shown. But I was definitely attracted to the man I met at the nightclub and wouldn't mind getting to know much more about him.

RICHARD

"This is no laughing matter Bee. This guy wants to see you again," stressed Sophie, and looking at me as if she had no other choice.

We were both alone at the front desk when she mentioned that statement to me. She was referring to Richard. Mr Richard Luke, to be exact. Sophie, whose boyfriend is a very good friend of Richard, introduced me recently to him. We were at the trendy nightclub in town, Zinc. It was a night out with some of the girls from front desk and reservations. They have been turning me into a party animal, which I didn't mind at all. After all, Alvin and I were no longer seeing each other. Plus, I was really pissed off about the real reason why we were no longer together. Going out with the girls from time to time, feels and seems like a good option.

It's really strange how one's feelings about something or someone can change so soon. When I broke up with Alvin, I certainly didn't expect to go man hunting, at least not in a rush. Besides, I wasn't the kind of girl who would chase after guys. But lately, I began to think that maybe I should! When I was introduced to Richard, I must admit , that he did have an effect on me right away! At first, I also thought that he was just another handsome fella, luring young women to his love nest, but I could be regretting saying that later, but I didn't feel that was the case with Richard. But realistically Belinda, who am I to be a judge of that!

No matter what evening of the week we decided to go to Zinc, Richard was always there, except when he was away on business. When he was there, he always acted like a gentleman.

Richard must have spoken to Sophie about me. She was always teasing me about him, especially when were alone.

"Well, Sophie, can we go to Zinc tomorrow night? Hopefully your friend, or should I say, our friend Richard , will be there."

"Trust me, Belinda, he will there," Sophie sounded very convinced.

And she was right too. When we got to the club, Richard was already there and had reserved a table in the lounge for a party of four. Sophie's boyfriend came along as well. Before we were seated, a waitress came by with a bottle of champagne, popped it open, and poured some into the four champagne glasses on the table. I was impressed with the surprise and presentation, which I concluded, was well planned in advance. This time around, I could be the judge of that!

Sophie was very smart too. I don't think she and her boyfriend had spent ten minutes at the table before she encouraged him to accompany her on the dance floor. The DJ was playing slow music. She suspected that I would not want to go on the dance floor to dance to some slow music that permeated the atmosphere. Plus, she knew Richard would prefer sitting at the table to have a conversation with me especially when no one else was around.

"So did you have a good day Belinda?" Richard, who had just taken another sip of champagne, asked me politely as soon as he realised that both Sophie and Wendel were locked arms around each other on the dance floor.

"It was okay," I responded, trying not to look or sound timid.

"And how was yours?" I reciprocated

"Could be better, but that's the way life is sometimes," he answered.

Richard and I got to know each other better that night. In fact, we spent an hour and a half getting acquainted. While he talked, I noticed so much about him, that if I hated him from just bouncing into him on a street, I would have had to change my mind now. Now that I met him in person and have spoken to him, I felt a connection. And yes, I was still sober. I barely had drunk the glass of champagne the waitress poured for me! But on a serious note, I felt completely different with Richard than when I met Alvin. Maybe it was because I didn't have a boyfriend then that I didn't rush into anything with Alvin. I know that I wouldn't be as cautious with Richard like I was with Alvin.

On that night, Richard never said anything about wanting a relationship with me, but my intuition told me he did! I felt it. I hoped he was reserving that question for our next encounter, a dinner date for next week that I gladly accepted. I couldn't wait!

I danced that night at Zinc nightclub like I had done it all my life. Richard wasn't a great dancer but I didn't care. All I wanted, was to be close to this tall and handsome man, who was already making me feel special. Sophie and her boyfriend joined us several times on the dancefloor and brought us champagne each time. I didn't want to drink more than three glasses of champagne. I was afraid of becoming tipsy and embarrass myself in front of the man I was starting to like very much. Richard, on the other hand, had more than seven glasses and still looked sober! It was obvious that he is used to drinking champagne.

I never imagined that a married man would mean so much to me. I remembered how upset I was when I learned that my mother was seeing a married man. The older folks would always remind us that part in the bible which says 'who God has joined together, let no man put asunder.'

They would sternly warn that 'anyone who gets between two married people, would feel the wrath of God. I didn't know what exactly the wrath of God looks like as judging from my mother's past involvement with a married man. don't think she has felt his wrath. Or, hmm, has she? Not quite sure of that coming to think of it. And I really would not like anything bad to happen to her since she has changed her past behaviour and is taking good care of my younger siblings.

According to Richard, he was married once. In his case, it's different because he was recently divorced. Though he is a few years older than me, I would definitely not hesitate to say 'yes,' if he desires to have a relationship with me.

Richard recalled that his four year marriage with some woman from Trinidad was more bad than good. He gave credit to his former wife though for being a good mother to their three year old son, Daniel. It was from that evidence that the court awarded her custody of him. Richard expressed his regrets over that. He was unable to see his son as often as he wished since his ex wife eventually moved by to Trinidad. According to him, the day after she was awarded custody of their son, she apparently returned to the house while he was at work and took every single thing that was moveable from the house!

Richard shook his head and said that the only thing that the woman left in the house, were the tiles on the floor and the wallpaper! She even took the only two framed photos he had of his parents and all his clothes! I was overwhelmed with disbelief as to what I heard and what his ex wife had done to him. However, I didn't want to get into something that frankly was not my business and because from our conversation, Richard said that he's gotten over all of that. My desire is to possibly start a relationship with this man and endeavour to make him happy within my own capabilities and efforts.

Sophie couldn't wait to return to work before she continued to tease me about Richard. She and Richard have obviously spoken since we last met at Zinc. She called me at work on her

days off to tell me that Richard was 'crazy about me.' I wasn't surprised but felt somewhat 'giddy in love,' knowing sooner rather than later, Richard and I would become lovers. Forgive me father but I cannot wait for that! Very possible, we both have been thinking the same within our own minds but the actual words or proposal has not yet been spoken. I pretended though I wasn't aware that Richard and I were slowly falling in love.

When Sophie asked me again what I thought of him, I gave her a casual and unexpected response.

"Like you can fool me Bee. The way you and Richard were looking at each other in the club the last time. I'm sure it was the beginning of the inevitable," Sophie said confidently. She was convinced that it would be just a matter of time before I confirm that Richard has now become my new boyfriend.

I never told Sophie that since I gave Richard my telephone that he's been calling me everyday. She would have loved too hear that but somehow, I sensed that she knew and that was why she continued to tease me about Richard.

Richard understood when I told him that it was best if he didn't come to my aunt's house to pick me up whenever we planned to go out. I didn't feel comfortable and was bursting with a bit of reluctance for him to see where I was living. My aunt's house was not in the best condition, even from the outside. They have recently added a bathroom but there was still much work to be done, including re painting both the internal and external areas. Furthermore, I didn't wish to arouse anyone's suspicion in the neighbourhood, particularly my aunt. I wanted to be absolutely certain that Richard and I will have established a relationship. I am aware too that after Richard and I decide to have a relationship, he would have to get used to my humble dwelling place. By contrast, he lives alone on his parents' estate on the north of the island.

Richard's parents were no longer alive. His two other elder brothers, both reside in England with their wives and children. Richard drives a luxury car too and works as a sales and marketing manager at a renowned paint company, which apparently was established more than fifty years ago. From time to time, he has the privilege of travelling to most of the Caribbean islands and infrequently to the states and Canada, to promote the company's products or as a representative at seminars or workshops.

I remembered him saying how happy he was whenever he got the chance to travel to Trinidad because he would get a chance to see his son.

"Daniel warms my heart everything I see him," Richard would say to me, registering a tone of a caring dad too.

Richard and I dined at Chez Solange, a French restaurant, located on a hilltop near a beach called Red Bay, on the southern side of the island. The cuisine was excellent and so was the service. At the end of the night, I wasn't surprised by the amount on the bill. Richard could tell that I was enjoying the ambience of the place and promised to that it was the first of many more visits. I didn't mind that at all. I feel safe with him and he could take me anywhere, except to meet the devil of course!

I had just taken the last bite of a very delicious French chocolate cake and had already lifted up my glass for another sip of red wine when Richard announced calmly but with a serious tone, " Belinda, I'm in love with you and I hope you're in love with me too. "

I blushed and blinked my eyes as if I was blind all my life and suddenly, I was now able to see. I took an extra sip of red wine and without any further delay, also let him know I am happily in love with him. With that news, Richard smiled, more broadly and shamelessly. He made a sign of the cross, got up from his chair and came forward to kiss me on my forehead.

That made me shiver with excitement. That night, we agreed to start a relationship and make the best out of it, come what may! That night too, I told Richard about everything about my life so far. When I finished, he showed compassion, picked up a napkin and wiped his eyes. It was no pretence. That made me shed some tears too. I excused myself from his company temporarily and headed to the ladies, where I locked myself inside a cubicle and cried some more. I was crying also for my new -found happiness, having seen a man shed tears for my past sorrows. And I was crying for the memories of my own past.

When I mentioned to Richard about the type of house I share with my aunt and her husband, he replied, "Whether or not you live in a hut, a mud house or wherever, I don't care; you're beautiful and I sense also that your heart is clean. That's more important to me," Richard assured and lifted my confidence that same night.

"I love you, Belinda and I fell in love with you from the very first time I laid my eyes on you."

I was feeling the same way about him, but I didn't reveal that to him. I didn't want another man to take me for another easy ride. Richard didn't appear to be that type of guy, but a woman, burnt once, has to be more careful going forward with another relationship.

I purchased a book from Minta's store that sells just about everything. You can find poultry, stationery, clothing and liquor, all jumbled up in this cramped store at the corner of Dark Alley in the village. Chin Fin, the owner, looked at me one day while I was in his shop and said, 'pretty girl, good book for you .' The book is entitled ,20 WAYS TO LOVE. It was written by some English psychologist, whose name looked more difficult to pronounce than Chin Fin's name. From observation, it entails a lot of values about true love. I believe it could help Richard and I in our relationship.

This time I telephoned Sophie and announced the news, or was it now? That Richard and I confirmed our relationship on our last dinner date. Sophie laughed with excitement in her voice and congratulated me. She expressed that she had been expecting to hear that announcement sooner. Everything Sophie predicted so far, came into being. She wished both Richard and me all the best in our new relationship and concluded that Richard would take very good care of me.

I was still reluctant to let my aunt and mother know that I have found a new man. I couldn't figure out the actual reason by delaying in letting them know. I noticed a similar pattern when I first started dating Alvin. Nonetheless, I wasn't ready to let them know. But my aunt wasn't stupid either. Many times when Richard called for me, she would be the one who would answer the phone. Richard was just about the only male who would phone the house and requests to speak with me. Obviously, my aunt has gotten used to hearing Richard's voice over the telephone. Eventually, out of the blue one night, after I had just finished speaking with Richard on the phone, my aunt asked as I appeared in the living room, "Bee, is that man your boyfriend?" I wasn't shocked by her question, but I was not expecting her to ask me that. I couldn't lie to her this time, so I told her the truth.

"Is he the one who's brought you home quite a few times in that nice white care?" my aunt further questioned. When I told her he's the one, my aunt didn't look upset, but she appeared somewhat surprised and left cold by the news, Then she muttered, "I hope he's not a married man, Bee."

"No aunty, He's divorced. I know he's older than me but so far, he's very much in love with me and treats me very well," I replied, almost politely defensive.

What I wanted to tell my aunt about Richard came out quite nicely. She understood and added that she cares about me and my well -being, especially in a relationship.

"After what Alvin did to you, I just didn't want another relationship that you find yourself in to be short lived," My aunt pointed out.

This time, I didn't give my aunt the chance to tell my mother about my new boyfriend before me. I telephoned her one evening and told her all about it. She sounded happy for me but mentioned that she hoped I wasn't rushing into something I would regret later. Like her sister, she didn't want me to meet another Alvin. Mother also gave me some good news that same evening. My brother and sisters would be coming to visit me in a matter of days! I was brought to tears by that announcement. From the excitement in my voice, my aunt who was nearby, guessed what it was all about. Everything good seemed to be happening to me all at once!

The big day finally came. I had a day off too. Richard took me to the airport to pick up my beloved ones. We had to wait an extra hour because the flight was delayed. When it finally arrived and brought my younger siblings safely, I looked towards the heavens and thanked God for their safe journey back to the island of their birth. I hugged and kissed my siblings over and over again. I was extremely delighted to see them. They all are grown up now. Even Samantha is taller than me now! When they confessed that they have missed their big sister, I was moved. I just couldn't help it. It was a mixture of tears and joy, seeing them in person after a while.

Our aunt and husband were already waiting outside the house for our return with our new guests. Both Richard and uncle Vincent helped to unload the luggage from the car while aunty

hugged and welcomed her nieces and nephew, thanking God for bring them home safely. When I got a chance, I officially introduced Richard to my aunt and her husband.

While my siblings were visiting us, many people became quite fond of them. Both Richard and uncle Vincent were especially fond of Jason. They both remarked how very

127

well- mannered he is and think that he is heading in the right direction for a young boy at his age. My aunt and Sophie loved my sisters. On few occasions, Sophie took the girls over to her house where they spent the night there most of the times. She even took all of them to the children's carnival parade in town.

My siblings loved the beach so whenever Richard was free from work, he took us to several beaches where we picnicked all day long. As always, we enjoyed ourselves to the fullest.

I couldn't count the number of times our mother called to speak, especially with her younger children while they were on vacation. At one point, I had to tell her that we were actually taking very care of her little ones! I don't think mother doubted that but it was evident that she has become very attached to them since they all left to reside in St Thomas. So, it was expected that she would have missed their presence.

When the day came for their departure, I cried again, and always hitting the trend to being a very emotional person. I was already missing my siblings terribly, more than I ever had! My aunt too, could not conceal her emotions, She and her husband accompanied us to the airport. This time, my thoughtful boyfriend, hired a family van to make it possible for everyone to take the journey in one vehicle. Uncle Vincent promised my siblings that he and his wife would come to visit them soon. He also gave then five American dollars each and urged them to continue to do well with their studies in school.

We waited until the aircraft disappeared in the clouds before we returned home. Later that day, mom telephoned to tell us that the children arrived back in St Thomas safely and already had been sharing their 'wonderful vacation,' according to them, with her. Mother even asked in some fits of laughter, what we were feeding the kids with during their five week stay, She commented that everyone one of them looked like they have gained a few extra pounds.

One night while I was getting ready to close off from the front desk at work and was just about to call Richard to me up, a female guest, who appeared to be in her late thirties, and who was definitely high on something, came up to the desk and demanded that I find her a man, a black man she then stressed. I wanted to burst out laughing but I couldn't, at least not in front of the guest.

CLINTON BENJAMIN

I kindly informed the guest that unfortunately it was a request that I couldn't possibly assist her with. She still didn't understand, looking strangely more perplexed by my response. So, she began to make her personal request and demand much louder. A bellboy, whom others have claimed that he likes female tourists, would have heard the guest since he was in the lobby and not too far away from the front desk. He tried to signal to me with some indicative gestures, but I pretended I didn't see and never acknowledged an approval. In the end, I managed to get away from the guest by telling her that I was going to look for a special number that she could call for further assistance but instead exited from the back office. I saw her the following day, sober as ever but was walking very differently. She didn't say a word to me. In fact, she walked passed the front desk and didn't look in its direction.

But I found out later that something allegedly had happened that night when she came to the front desk with her strange request. That same bellboy called me aside one day after I clocked off from work and said, "Pardon me, friend, but I gave it to her that night until I knocked the rum out of her! Until she screamed, no, no, no more !"

I laughed and laughed until Sophie came by to find out if I was okay. When I discreetly told her why I was laughing like that, she couldn't help but cracked up laughing much more than I did!

There were other instances at the front desk that would make me either become concerned or laugh about the situation. I recalled an American man, around forty, who came to the front desk, one evening while Sophie and I were there. He pleaded for one of us to go to his suite where he was staying with wife and speak with her. According to the male guest, his wife revealed that she has fallen in love with a native rastaman, whom she met on a day boat cruise, and informed her husband that was not going back to America! Eventually, Sophie did speak with the man's wife, who did verify her husband's claim. However, in the end, she returned to America with her husband and her rastaman friend! Sophie and I never learned what actual arrangements the couple came to from his initial concern , and especially under what conditions the husband consented for the rastaman to return with him and his wife to America. We really would have liked to know.

My honey bunch, Richard, started teaching me how to drive. At first, I was a bit apprehensive but he encouraged me to brave, even at times when I knew I was doing poorly at the wheels. I eventually got the hang of it and when he was satisfied, he signed me up to take the exams, which I passed at one attempt! Still, I wasn't ready to drive a car of my own. Sophie congratulated me for having obtained my driver's license with one attempt.

Her boyfriend was not too keen to teach her to drive. That made me feel profoundly proud of Richard for having taken time and patience to teach me. I keep appreciating him more and more, every single day.

I couldn't resist making love with Richard. We first went out that evening to our favourite nightclub, Zinc. Just him and I. We were all alone and loved very minute of it. We drank together, danced together and definitely had a fantastic time at the club. I spent the night at his house. This man, my man is a great lover, although I couldn't get over his massive manhood. That was not an understatement, as seeing is believing! The thought has now crossed my mind, thinking if I am the lucky or unlucky one who keeps finding boyfriends with these mini like snakes, to say the least! I am now tempted to find out from my friend Sophie if her boyfriend is also gifted in that area.

Thank God Andy finally called! I was unable to reach him whenever I telephoned him and was becoming a bit concerned, especially when it was his answering machine, with some funny pre-recorded message I got . It made me laugh every time: 'Greetings, brethren and sistering- I and I vibes is out. Any message-release your speech after the beep.'

Mother also said she had tried a few times to get in touch with Andy but never got through. When I told my brother about our experiences trying to get in touch with him, he explained that he and his wife were staying at her parent's place during the last few weeks of the pregnancy and a few more weeks after her delivery. His voiced was filled with a joyous tone as he proudly announced that is now a father.

"Jah gave us a healthy and bouncing baby boy," he announced

I congratulated him and his wife and requested that he gives their baby, my little nephew a kiss for me.

Their son weighed nine pounds at birth. He was named after his father. When Andy told me that, I joked and asked him if the baby also carries his middle name. He laughed, knowing the very reason I asked. I saw Andy's birth certificate once and noticed an unusual name which I was unable to pronounce until grandpa told me how, NI-CO-DE-MUS. I laughed hysterically that my mother responded that she should have actually made my middle name to be JEZEBEL. After her revelation, I didn't quite find that idea to be funny at all.

My brother did confirm that his son's full name is actually Andy, Nicodemus Jr. Before we hung up the phone, he promised that he was also going to call mother and give her the great news of his newborn.

The thought of Andy being a father made me think deep about wanting to have kids some day. It wouldn't be six or seven children like I see many young women in the village doing. That would be too much for me to handle. I believe two or three would be fine but no more than that! I pray for no twins or triplets, although I do adore seeing them. I would wish to have one child per pregnancy. Richard would also like to have more children but said he wanted to get married before that happens. I agree with him. I didn't plan to be a single parent. I would like the father of my children to be present in their upbringing.

It was a beautiful evening, the full moon was out in its glory, shining its silvery light on the atlantic ocean. Richard insisted that we find a suitable spot on a beach while we drove along the western coast of the island. And that we did. He just wanted a quiet place where we could sit in the car, talk and listen to soulful music. We talked about so many things. One topic lead to another until the conversation got quite steamy. He held my hands and guided them to his already bulged area. My mouth became fully stuffed. It was a first for me. I felt awkward but

Richard must have enjoyed it as he moaned with pleasure while I on the other hand, welcomed some fresh air once my mouth was vacant again!

I was overwhelmed with joy when Richard presented me with an engagement ring one night as we dined at Chez Solange. We never discussed marriage in depth so I was a bit surprised, yet delighted.

"Bee, as he now calls me most of the times, you are the woman I want to spend the rest of my life with." As usual, I was close to tears. I held on to my man, my future husband and let him know that I would be happy to be his woman for life. With that revelation, he kissed me and embraced me tightly. Finally, when he brought me back home that night and I was all alone, I began to hear wedding bells. I began planning the wedding all in my head, thinking who would give me away, my bridesmaid and all that. I didn't want to get too caught up in counting my chickens before they are hatched. For, I have heard or read stories of women being engaged for years but never got married. Personally speaking, I don't think that I would have the patience to wait on any man for more than two years when he would be still thinking then if he should marry me. Sophie agreed with me too when I voiced my opinion of that. She opened her eyes wider and put one hand over her mouth when she saw the ring on my finger and remarked, "Bee, you're not easy. You're one lucky woman. Congratulations!"

The girls at the office started to make plans for a staff Christmas party. They did so every year. Apparently, management allocates a certain amount each year and the girls from reservations and front desk usually plan the event. We also organized a gift exchange for interested work colleagues.

The week leading up to the Christmas holidays was as hectic as ever. I helped my aunt cleaned the entire house. It was the only time that the house got such thorough cleaning. Mother had already sent us some goodies for Christmas, along with some curtains for the

living room and kitchen. My aunt was quite fascinated with all of the preparations for Christmas. Like most people, she baked cakes, cooked ham and roasted the biggest turkey I ever saw! She also made ginger beer and sorrel drink with the intention of serving any visitor who would pass by during the festive holidays.

I could only afford to buy gifts for four people. The others I sent or gave Christmas cards. I bought my dear Richard a lovely aftershave, a watch for Sophie and a Science textbook for John. I presented my aunt with a nice white cotton dress which fitted her perfectly.

Christmas day was an extra special day for me, for it was on that day around the dinner table that he asked me to marry him, officially. I had a piece of cake in my mouth when he made that announcement in the presence of my aunt and uncle. I almost choked!

Richard has gotten used to my aunt's place, so when she invited him around for Christmas dinner, he didn't turn down her offer. My aunt and I tried out best to the put the house in near perfect order but doubt if that would have made any difference to my boyfriend's natural understanding of the situation. He gets along with just about anyone. My aunt grinned from ear to ear when she heard Richard's announcement and wished us all the best. Later on, when he and I were alone, we further discussed plans for our wedding day. We both agreed to have our wedding day on his birthday, the twentieth of March. He would be thirty-five and expressed that he would have so much to celebrate on that day.

We planned to have a medium sized wedding with no more than a hundred and fifty guests. The reception would be held on his parents' estate, in their backyard garden, which gives a beautiful view of the sea on one side and of a gorgeous mountain on the other side. Richard wanted his older brother, Simon, to be his best man while I was hoping Andy would be the one who walks me down the aisle. That meant I would have to inform him at my soonest so I

would know in due course. I planned on having both my younger sisters and Sophie as my bridesmaids. There would be lots of preparations before that day so we both agreed to start organising right away.

Mother couldn't believe it when I told her about the wedding. While she admitted that she was elated of the news, she did confess that she didn't expect to hear of one soon. Sophie said the same thing. Both women have offered to support me as much as they possibly could. Mother hinted that she would definitely be at the wedding under every circumstances, even saying she wouldn't care if she has to steal the money to buy the airline tickets in order to attend my wedding. She obviously was joking. She believes that her boss, a boutique owner, would lend her whatever amount of money she needed if she was unable to source the funds elsewhere.

Andy too expressed a pleasant shock when I revealed to him that I was getting married. I couldn't blame him. Don't think that I had ever mentioned to him that I was dating someone nor could I recall ever him asking me anything to do with that or men.

"Sis, anything for you," was my brother's response when I asked him if he would be able to travel to this side of the world sooner than he expected, to walk his sis down the aisle. He wasn't certain if his wife and child would be able to though. But he assured me that he was going to make reservations to fly out a few days before the wedding day as soon we got off of the telephone.

Aunt Lyn invited my boyfriend and I to an old year's church service. She reminded us that it was a good way to end the year and start a new one. We took up the invitation although I was tempted to attend an old year's party that Sophie had invited us to.

But we would be receiving greater blessings by going to the church service than if we went out drinking. We had been doing that all year long. My aunt does have a valid point.

Late January, I was transferred to the reservations department. I also received confirmation from management that I was now an established employee of the resort. The transfer wouldn't be definite until I return from my vacation in the second week of March. I didn't mind either way as both reservations and the front desk are under the same roof. I would still be able to see the girls from front desk.

I planned to request extra time away from work so that I would be able to attend more freely to the many necessary obligations before and after the wedding.

Sophie volunteered to print the wedding invitation cards. Richard and I began handing some out and mailed the rest to other invited guests in the last week of January. Sophie recommended her seamstress to make my wedding gown and the clothes for the rest of the bridal party, except Richard's. When Sophie introduced me to her seamstress, I didn't like her that much at first because she never stopped talking and barely gave me a chance to explain certain details to her. And quite frankly too nosey for me. Sophie agreed with me but emphasized that she does a great job and that I can trust her on that. I didn't doubt Sophie for one bit as I often complimented her for some stunning outfits I have seen her worn and to which she always proudly said that she does have a great seamstress. And for that, I trusted Ms Tonge to do what she seemed to do best, designing and sewing clothes with a uniqueness to each piece she's created.

One of the girls at work made a silly remark that made me wanted to kick her in her behind, literally. Don't think she was aware that I was in one of the ladies' cubicles in the rest room when she referred to my husband to be as an old man and said that I was probably marrying him because I wanted to move in with him in the big house on his parents' estate. Everybody in the office knows that lazy Renee -Floyd is a damn nosey and mouthy charlatan. She was always minding other people's business and forgetting hers. It was rumoured that she wore an engagement ring for over two years and was forced to take it off in the end. The man who gave her the engagement ring, apparently dumped her to marry her cousin instead. When I appeared, she was shocked to see me that she couldn't utter another word. She finally came up with the nerves to ask me how my wedding was coming along. I just walked out of the restroom like she wasn't even there. Even though I brought a general invitation card for the front desk and reservations staff, I simply do not want to see Renee-Floyd at my wedding or else I would personally ask her to leave!

Uncle Vincent and four other persons won the lottery during last week's draw. Sixty thousand dollars were to be shared among the four winners. Though my aunt was against gambling, she did tell her husband that the money he won came at the right time. It would certainly help them with their planned trip to St Thomas, later in the year. They could also dress like a king and queen on my wedding day. My aunt also wanted her husband to use some of his winnings 'to fix up' the house a little before our guests arrived, mother and siblings. Poor uncle Vincent, as if he had won millions, was offering some money to me to help out with the wedding plans he said. But I politely refused it. And he wasn't offended. My fiancé has already planned to foot the bill to all matters relating to our wedding.

My aunt finally got in touch with her brother Arthur. She was told that he has been arrested by the police for allegedly beating up his girlfriend. My aunt was really worried about that news and had already gone to his residence several times, but he wasn't there. The house, according to her looked abandoned.

Uncle was upset by the rumour that he had been arrested. According to him, he had gotten completely fed up of Bernita's attitude and told her to leave the house for which he alone was paying the rent and utilities. She refused to leave so eventually, he went to the police station to make a report on her. Uncle Arthur recalled how Bernita was behaving so badly at the police station, that one policewoman was convinced she was having a nervous breakdown.

"And what about the kids?" my aunt questioned her brother.

"Oh, I'm still looking after them," he replied with assurance.

"Great. I am glad you are no longer seeing Bernita anymore. Our God works in mysterious ways. Don't you think so?" my aunt waited for an answer from her brother.

My aunt was pleased with her brother's decision but was a bit concerned why he never stopped by to let her know. As usual, uncle Arthur apologized and promised that he would keep in contact with his sister on a regular basis from now on. I also informed him of my wedding day, an announcement that surprised him.

"Of course, I'll be there and if you need a bartender, please let me know," uncle Arthur replied. He also left his telephone number before he departed to catch a bus to take him to Coconut Town, a larger village than Ponds, around sixteen miles from it.

Meanwhile, my aunt was on her knees thanking God for having delivered her brother from the wicked hands of Bernita. She used that opportunity to pray for the rest of the family that they may soon turn their lives over to Christ before it was too late.

Our wedding day was just weeks away. As the time gets closer, I was becoming more and more nervous. Richard had already purchased our wedding rings. We ordered then from a special catalogue along with his tuxedo.

We even had less worries thinking about the catering. His employer volunteered to sponsor the entire catering including the decoration and staffing, a very kind gesture from them for which we are eternally grateful.

The wedding ceremony will be held at Richard's church, The Methodist Chapel in the city, something we both agreed on.

The seamstress has already completed ninety percent work on the order. The excitement was truly building for what we anticipate to be a wonderful and memorable day for me and my darling fiancé.

Mother and my younger siblings were the first ones to arrive at the house. It was a very happy moment for me to see them again. Mother looked much younger in person than in the pictures she sent some months ago. She was even boasting about what the gym has been doing to her. Andy arrived three days later. He was very tired the day he arrived since he travelled more than eleven hours. He went straight to bed when he got to the house.

Aunt Lyn was delighted to see them all thanked the Lord for their safe journey home. Both she and her sister chatted incessantly. I never realized how much marijuana Andy actually smokes. He has already reunited with some of his old friends and who, were definitely supplying him with weed galore. Sometimes he would go to the back of the yard to an isolated spot and according to him, smokes and meditates. He sported long dreadlocks, which look very healthy.

March twentieth finally came upon us. It was a perfect day with no forecast that it was going to rain. It was raining a bit the day before, which got me a bit worried, but the sun finally came up in the later afternoon. And again, on our wedding day, the sun came out in all of its glory.

The bridal party, excluding Richard of course, had to be dressed at the seamstress. Sophie got her sister and another friend of hers to be the makeup artists and dressers. They did a magnificent job, including the seamstress. We arrived at the church on time. Richard was already there as were most of our guests. As expected, there were some onlookers outside the church, staring at me and my wedding dress, making their own personal comments among themselves.

"Wow! What a lovely princess," whispered one guy as I walked up the steps to the church entrance with the bridal party behind of me. As funny as that might sound, that particular comment said in that moment, calmed some of my nervousness.

The ceremony got on the way. Richard looked so charming and handsome in his black tuxedo. My heart was beating heavily. I took a deep breath. That helped.

When the moment came for us to take our vows, I ensured that I was listening attentively, so I didn't say the wrong thing or say Richard's full name incorrectly. I did well with that in the end. And so did my man, who has now officially become my husband. My handsome hubby drew back the veil over my head and kissed me with his warm lips when the minister gave him the honours to kiss his bride. I became Belinda Olivia Luke and felt immensely proud of my new last name. My husband showered me with endless attention and introduced me to many of his work colleagues, especially at the reception. We took pictures galore, with friends and family and also with people that I have never met or seen before.

The moment for the speeches came. They were both hilarious and moving. Andy, my aunt and my mother were the first ones to speak on my behalf. My mother spoke like she didn't want to stop. She told the gathering that she was very proud of her daughter. She made me giggled because she at times she was speaking in a deep 'Thomian' accent, which was barely easy to understand. Mother definitely had been drinking and that's okay. She was allowed to celebrate her daughter's big day and new life with her son in law.

Richard's brother, Simon, was too much for me. He was very eloquent, too posh. He spoke like another Shakespeare and evoked a romantic setting when he recited a piece from Shakespeare's work. Richard's boss, an aunt of his and some of his friends, including Sophie's boyfriend, Wendell, spoke well of him. But it was John and Sophie who surprised me the most by rendering a duet especially for us. It made me shivered with excitement and I was touched by their efforts. I never knew they both could sing so beautifully. I also wondered how and when they planned that!

The MC ordered everyone to find a seat as dinner was about to be served.

After everyone got served dinner and desserts and were settled at their tables, my husband and I made our entrance to the dancefloor. The feeling was indescribable. We moved to the slow rhythm. My husband whispered in my ears a few times telling me that he will cherish me forever. I assured him too that we will make the marriage work as we remain loving and faithful to each other until death do us part. Our guests were invited on to the dancefloor which became packed with many of guests dancing to the tunes that our DJ was playing. I danced with just about everyone of my family in attendance, including uncle Vincent , who boogied down to calypso music and was doing a fine job. His wife just stared at him in disbelief but with a content look in the end.

When the night's celebration was over and most of our guests had left, Richard and I were driven away to a nearby hotel where we were going to spend the night. He surprised me when we got there by showing me two airline tickets to the French island of Martinique.

I was under the impression that we would have our honeymoon a bit later in the year. Instead, we would be leaving the next day to Martinique to spend four nights there.

Our time spent there was incredible and unforgettable. The love we have for each other was on full display and neither of us were reluctant for a snog on the streets on Fort de France or spent the whole day in bed on our first night.

I reminisced the very first time my husband and I stepped into the hotel's restaurant, hand in hand, my head resting on his shoulder, using it as a temporary pillow. When we were seated, a very tall gentleman came over to our table. Yes, he was handsome but not more than my prince. His accent was incredibly strong and romantic.

"May eye elp you?" and then after we had our dinner, he returned to our table and said with a thin smile, "You will av a bottle of wine on da owse!"

My husband knows how to speak French in basic conversations, but I discovered on our honeymoon, he didn't know much to save our lives! We both found it very amusing when I wanted to say good morning in French and said 'banjo!'

"No honey, its 'bon-joo (bonjour), my husband carefully corrected me in laughter.

"It better be that because what would a musical instrument has to do with greetings in any language," I thought to myself.

Another time we misunderstood the maid. We misunderstood the very little English she knew to mean otherwise when she said, "Zere ist shit on za bed!" She too had a very strong French accent and it slipped that sentence off of her tongue, like English was spoken like that. In one quick reaction, we wondered what 'shit' could be on the bed and why would she be telling us

that anyway. Eventually, we realised that she was referring to a new sheet that she had not too long ago, spread on our bed!

The French island of Martinique is a very beautiful place, almost like a French metropolitan in the Caribbean. The roads are well constructed, but the drivers seemed to be always in a hurry. Always exceeding the speed limit. While we were there, another motorist almost ran into the rent-a-car we hired. It was my husband's quick defensive driving that freed and saved us from what could have been a fatal accident.

My husband and made love to me in broad daylight while we were having a bath in one of the lovely and many rivers Martinique is blessed with. The river is located in the heart of a hilly area on the north eastern side of the island called Les Chateaux D'Herbre. We were the only visitors there at the time. A heavy shower came down on us. We loved every drop of it! What a soak it was.

When we got back from our honeymoon, Andy and Richard's brother had already left for their respective homes. Andy couldn't spend that much time way from his wife and son. He wanted to be there to assist his wife with their child. Simon who's a professor, had to return earlier because of his obligations to the university where he works. Mother and my other siblings were due to leave in a few days. My mother didn't want the children to be away from school for too long.

While we were on our honeymoon, they all did a good job putting away all the wedding gifts and the wedding cake. They even cleaned Richard's house, my new home too. I had already packed most of my belongings before the wedding so there wasn't much left to do. A massive thank you to the organizing and cleaning crew.

I sensed too that my aunt was going to miss me when I move to my new residence. It made me felt a bit nostalgic thinking about it. One thing I promised to do, is to visit them whenever I can or speak with them on the telephone. I was going to miss Ponds in so many ways, where I witnessed good and some bad times. I am glad that I have a loving husband who is my rock and human comforter. I know he would continue to encourage me to look ahead positively and to disallow the past to be a stumbling block for the happiness and I desire.

My mother, and all of my siblings were going to spend the night at my new residence before they depart for St Thomas. Having them overnight with us, would make it easier for my husband to take them to the airport in the morning.

Aunt Lyn was quite emotional as she said goodbye to her sister, nieces and nephew. When mother was finished embracing her, I gave my aunt a hug too, kissed her and requested that she prays for all of us. My aunt was still very teary as she promised to do so. Mother became an emotional wreck. She embraced her sister again. They hugged for a longer time, promising they would communicate with each other as often as possible.

Before we drove my aunt back to Ponds, she reminded her sister about the visit she and her husband were planning to St Thomas, later in the year. That moment brought both of them some joy, knowing that they will be seeing each other sister soon again.

Mother replied, "Sis, we'd be very happy to see you anytime."

My dear husband put his arms and around me and reassured me that everything was going to be okay when he saw some tears falling uncontrollably down my cheeks.

"Cheer up sweetheart. I understand your feelings right now as saying goodbye to the ones you love dearly, is never an easy experience for most people." My husband's words did

bring me some relief. I gave my aunt another hug and told her to convey our regards to her husband when he returns from work.

"Don't worry aunty. I'll come and visit you as often as possible," I reassured her.

"Okay dear. God bless you and your husband," she softly replied.

Richard also gave her a hug before we got into the car and drove back to Luke's estate, my new home.

The next day was going to be another emotional day for me because it was the actual day my mother and siblings were returning to St Thomas. I would have to get used to them being away from me and learn to live with my husband in peace, love and harmony. My siblings were getting older too and one day will have lives of their own to live. As their biggest sister, I would continue to look after their best interests and pray to God to guide and watch over them as He also guides me through my marriage.

When my mother and siblings departed St Thomas, my husband and I returned to the house to sort out many things there. It is a big house with three spacious bedrooms, two bathrooms and more domestic work for me. For the time being only Richard and I inhabit it. The babies would come later, adding understandably more chores to and more places to occupy.

I had to use the bathroom and while I was there, I paused also for a moment to reflect how lucky I am to have found such a wonderful man like Richard, who looked beyond my circumstances and loved enough to marry me. He looked further than my outer beauty and gradually invited me to share part of his heart, to share life with him until God calls one or both us home. All this once again overwhelmed me, so much so when I came out from the bathroom, I called my husband from wherever he was in the house. He arrived in seconds and when he was close enough to me, asked, "Were you calling me, honey?"

I gently replied, "Yes, sweetheart, I was calling you to thank you for marrying me and to tell you I will always love you for as long as you live."

He held my hands and took me to our bedroom. He had already been playing Barry White and the voice and the music were driving me romantically crazy.

"Let's make love sweetheart," Richard kindly suggested.

The music and the presence of my husband staring lusciously at me, made me want him again. As the excitement was escalating, the telephone rang but we disregarded it. Until it rang again, but I got slightly concerned with the persistent ringing of the phone.

"Oh Richie, maybe it's important. Can we pause for a sec and see who it is?"

"Okay, okay baby but no long conversations please, unless it's an emergency or of high importance, "my dear husband advised.

When I answered the phone, it was Sophie.

"Sorry Bee if I disturbed you guys," Sophie said, not sure how telepathic she actually is

"You got that right baby girl," I quickly replied, sounding unintentionally sarcastic.

"Well excuse me Mrs Luke. Night hasn't even fallen yet and you two are at it again?" Sophie asked while laughing.

"Well Sophie dear, we are now married so we can do it anytime without feeling any guilt. Doesn't matter what time of the day it is darling."

"Okay Mrs Luke. Wasn't calling you for any specific reason but now I know you're alright, I guess you can give a call whenever you're free," Sophie admitted.

"I'll call you later Sophie but for now, my husband's calling and he is waiting patiently for my return, to his arms." I turned the volume of the phone ringer to its lowest level so that we would not be disturbed again.

Barry White was singing the lines, 'telling you this, telling you that....' I was anxious for my husband to tell me more of his love. To give me more of his love. I opened the way for him and he gradually entered there without delay and with care.

When we were finally drained from out hot rendezvous, we showered together.

Richard volunteered to make us supper. We had steamed kingfish and a medley of vegetables including a favourite, cassava. It was sumptuous and cooked to perfection. Compliments to my husband's first cooking efforts. Truly, I was enjoying my married life so far. My darling Richard means so much to me and I was starting to think that it was a real possibility that I couldn't live without him.

WHERE THERE'S
AN END .....

Living on Luke's estate with my husband alone, was definitely a different experience than living at Ponds. The whole environment was different here. While at Ponds, I lived in a community where everyday life involved seeing vehicles, people going to and fro and noise everywhere. The Luke's estate, on the other hand, is a haven of tranquillity. Our closest neighbour lived about a mile away from the estate. And once in a while, a vehicle might pass by on the main road. There are no roosters around to signal the morning wake up call with their crowing, a routine familiar with village life. Richard has mentioned though that his parents used to have a variety of animals many years ago, including roosters, until a serious hurricane came and destroyed the entire flock. So, they didn't bother to start all over again.

Our backyard is home to many plants and flowers. Fruit trees such as mango, plum, orange and cherry, flourished in abundance. It reminded me of the plot of land my grandparents once had at Valley.

Sophie dropped by uninvited. She drove this time, unaccompanied and without a driver's license. It was her decision, so I didn't mind her dropping by. My husband was out. We sat in the back garden enjoying the beauty of nature around us , and chatting on about everything, including my wedding. She even mocked the way I sounded the last time she telephoned the house. I added no comments but laughed.

Sophie volunteered to assist me with the 'thank-you' notes for the guests who attended my wedding. I was grateful for that. Before she left, we both partook of some curried conch with white rice. She even advised that she would be visiting me again precisely in eight days' time.

I called my aunt the same evening to hear how she was doing.

"Oh Bee, I was just thinking of you and was planning to call," my aunt expressed as soon as she heard my voice.

"Well, I thought about you and your husband and decided to call ...."

"That's so sweet of you. We miss your company, but day by day, we are getting used to you not being here," my aunt solemnly stated.

I also invited my aunt and her husband, if he could, to spend the coming weekend with us but my aunt was concerned that she would miss out on her usual Sunday church service. My husband wouldn't mind dropping her off at the church on the Sunday morning, so I convinced her and she agreed to, also confirming her husband as well.

It was the first time that my aunt had a good view of the estate. They both marvelled at the vast acres of a well - kept estate. At least once a month, my husband would hire a group of men to clean the surrounding areas and manicure the lawn depending how tall the grass might have grown.

Uncle Vincent spent a lot of time in the back garden while me and my aunt reminisced about the wedding in the living room. She expressed how gorgeous I looked and that Richard was as handsome as ever in his tuxedo.

"Everything was well organised," she continued as we headed for the kitchen.

She wanted to do all the cooking while they spend the weekend with us. I was unable to convince my aunt that I would do some of it so that she could relax more, but she won eventually. In any case, my aunt is a fine cook and had asked me to tell her what we would like for dinner each day they were with us. I am looking forward for some sumptuous meals like coconut dumplings with stewed salt fish and vegetables, pepper pot and the likes. My husband also adores those types of meals. I can imagine how delighted he would be to be served those delicacies.

My aunt and husband enjoyed the weekend with us, so much so, that they have already given us a solid assurance that they will be back soon. They both were ready for their usual Sunday church service, so my husband transported them back to their home in time for it. I also suggested to my aunt that the next time they return to spend time with us, they are welcomed to stay longer and that all of us could attend Sunday worship together. She was very excited with that suggestion.

Richard finally brought home the pictures from our wedding day, fitted in two large picture albums. It had taken the photographer a longer time to get the films developed even though my husband had paid him extra money to have the pictures ready much sooner than normal. However, I was impressed with the pictures presented in the albums. My husband and I looked at them over and over again. I couldn't remember how many times he said, "Look at my beautiful princess."

Mark you, he looked like a handsome actor in the pictures. I had to let him know how photogenic he is. My husband was smart too, having asked the photographer to make some extra copies from the negatives. Of course, the photographer didn't charge him extra considering he took a longer period to give us the first sets of pictures.

We were planning of sending copies of our wedding pictures to close friends and to some of our immediate family members.

With my husband's consent, I had my hair cut into a different style, not to the extreme though. I wanted to sport a new look upon returning back to work.

The girls at the office were happy to see me again. Those who attended the wedding talked about the wonderful time they had. Renee-Floyd was the only one who had nothing to say because she wasn't invited after what scandalous thing I heard her gossiped about my fiancé then. I don't hate the person but I am being careful what I say in her presence because she would exaggerate on the contents.

Every Wednesday evenings, my husband, along with the guys from his office meet at some clubhouse in town to play dominoes. I was getting used to that. It was obvious that he enjoys playing the game which he said he has been playing for a long time. I have no intentions of being a miserable wife and discourage him from playing his dominoes. Only sometimes, I'd miss him for a few hours every Wednesday evening. What matters most is that whenever he returns, he still finds time to hug me, even sometimes when I was already asleep.

My friend, John, telephoned me one evening and expressed his excitement in taking his college exams within a few weeks.

" I am studying real hard Belinda," John said to me, sounding so positive as usual.

"I do believe you John and I'll be praying for you to," I responded.

He also mentioned that his girlfriend would also be taking the same exams. I wished both of

them good luck success in their exams. I even invited both of them to our house after they will have completed their exams.

In previous years, I was used to letting my birthday slipped by without even remembering until weeks after. It wasn't a big deal as there were so much going in my life that celebrating my birthday never crossed my mind back then. I believe that only twice I had ever received birthday cards. My husband must have noted the date because on that particular day, he presented me with a pleasant shock of my life!

"Happy birthday my wife, happy birthday my wife!" sang my husband to me that morning after he returned from the bathroom. It took me a few minutes to register that it was actually my birthday. My twenty-fourth as a matter of fact. It was a Saturday morning and coincidentally had the day off from work. My husband took me shopping and bought me two wonderful gifts, a gorgeous gold necklace and a whole line of beauty products. That same evening, we dined at our favourite restaurant, Chez Solange. The rest of the evening was spent behind closed doors, figuratively marked, 'private and engaged,' at our residence. The birthday could not have ended any better. Oh Richard, where do you get all that energy from?

We received the other sets of wedding pictures from the photographer and I picked a few to mail to my brother in Switzerland and my mother. Mother was the first one to call when she received the pictures to say she couldn't stop looking at them. She even told me how much she and my siblings laughed when they saw a picture of uncle Vincent boogying down on the dance floor at the reception. I clearly remembered that moment when the DJ was playing his favourite calypso music. I also spoke with my siblings who were very happy to see the memories of my wedding day, which they were also a part of, in pictures.

I also heard from Andy later in the week. He too was very impressed with the pictures and informed me that his wife now wished she had come to my wedding. I spoke with her too and she expressed how she was looking forward to meet me and the rest of the family when they travel to the Caribbean. Before we ended the phone call, I congratulated both of them for producing such an adorable and healthy looking baby boy. I recognised that from the pictures I recently received in the mail from my brother.

My husband had to leave the island for two days on company business. He was concerned about my staying alone on the estate, while he was away. I was okay being alone for two days but he suggested that someone stay with me while he was away for the two days. So Sophie volunteered but asked it was okay if Wendell joins her. Richard was also okay with that. Everything went fine, except on the second night, while I was lying in bed, Sophie rapped on the door. When I invited her in, she entered whispering, "Do you have any condoms?"

"Oh please girl, just go to bed you two. Can't you wait until tomorrow when you're back at your place?" I asked.

She left shamelessly but later in the night, I was awakened by some familiar noises coming from their bedroom. Didn't need a second guess as to what was happening there. In the morning, she begged to call work and report sick for her. Apparently, her left side was hurting her. I laughed to myself, 'serves her right!'

My husband and I surprised my aunt and her husband by joining them at their usual Sunday morning worship.

There were familiar faces there in attendance too. John and his mother were there and some other folks whom I have previously met either through John or my aunt. It was a good church service. I could see my husband was enjoying the lively music and songs, even though his denomination doesn't worship with such liveliness. My aunt introduced my husband to the pastor and a few other members of the congregation before we drove to her place for lunch.

We were treated to a hefty lunch of fried chicken in creole sauce. macaroni cheese and assorted vegetables on the side. While my husband found space in his stomach to accommodate the piece of potato pudding offered to us for dessert, I had to request that my aunt wrap mine up to take with me. I was too full to have anything else. Besides, I was watching my weight!

Time was fast approaching for my aunt and husband to take their dream holiday, according to them. My aunt had never been on an aircraft and she expressed some mixed feelings about being in one many thousand feet above ground. She has told me too that whenever she watches the news on TV and sees plane crashes, her fear of flying overtakes her. However, she is still determined to visit her sister in another island and that thought eases some of her anxieties. I had already gotten all of the US dollars they wanted to take on their vacation.

Uncle Vincent, on the other hand, was the happier of the two. He had ridden on a plane before, many years ago when his parents brought him to the island when he was a young boy.

"Going to St Thomas, is like going to a U S port ," he expressed frantically. I didn't ask him to elaborate on that but I have an idea why. St Thomas is part of the United States Virgin Islands, governed by the United States. They would be spending two months in St Thomas. Mother and my siblings have been eagerly awaiting their arrival. The day before the departed for St Thomas, my mother telephoned me, giving the same instructions she gave me numerous times in our previous calls. Her concern was that she would not like her sister and husband to encounter any unnecessary immigration problems when they land in St Thomas.

So I made certain I filled out the US Immigration card with the correct information in advance for the travelling couple.

The long awaited Friday morning came at last. My aunt and her husband were all dressed, their luggage were already outside the house when we got there to pick them up for the airport. On our way to the airport, the two confessed that they were unable to sleep and finally got out of bed around four to start to get ready for the trip.

Everything went smoothly at the airport. Their flight even departed on time for a change. My aunt has left their house keys with me so that I can keep an eye on things there whenever I can. We waited until the aircraft took off and was no longer in sight, before we returned home.

We both had enough time for a full breakfast before we got prepared and went to our separate jobs. I was early enough to take the staff bus to the hotel, so I didn't mind my husband dropping me off at the bus stop.

Not many staff turned up at work that day. Many were on strike, especially those who work in the housekeeping and kitchen departments. They are seeking an increase in their wages as well as seeking more staff benefits. I wasn't aware of their grievances and that it has reached the point of striking.

It was Sophie's day off. When I tried to telephone her, I got no reply. However, a lady who works in reservations filled me in with the latest developments of the strike.

Management apparently was not too pleased with the actions of the employees concerned and their union. They called for an urgent meeting with officials from the union with the hope of coming to an amicable agreement in the end. Some kind of progress was made after such

meeting and those who were on strike, were encouraged by their union representatives to return to their jobs as soon as possible. Things returned to normalcy, sooner than anticipated.

Everything went safe and well with my aunt and her husband. They had a smooth plane ride to St Thomas and did not have any problems going through US customs and immigration there. I did tell my mother even though I'd love to hear from her, she should call me only once a week or if there was something very important to share, then she should call sooner. My mother loves to make telephone calls. Although she gets good telephone rates on international calls, she always gets a huge bill each month because she was calling me and Andy very often as well as her other friends here and in the States.

My husband and I were in the mood to go disco dancing. We hadn't done so in long time. Sophie had begun calling me a housewife because most of the times she invited me out since I got married, I politely declined. Many of our friends were at the night club. It felt like the good old time again. We had a blast. My husband was dancing better this time. The atmosphere was electric. We left Zinc with a hot fever that we both had to cool ourselves down with a nice bath once we returned home.

I was at work one evening and while I was having my dinner break, Sophie rushed into the canteen and told me that I should call my husband immediately. I could sense that something was wrong. Just the by the way Sophie looked and rushed into the canteen. And her tone of voice too. She must have felt that after my husband telephoned her. I was panicking and felt very frightened. I rushed to the nearest phone and called my husband. My heart was beating faster than normal. I was also trembling both in my voice and body that I was slowly losing my balance, standing on my feet.

"My dear, it's very bad news," my husband said, breathing heavily over the phone.

"Oh my God, what is it Rich?" I quickly asked. Fright has completely taken me over.

"Please come home now darling. Take a taxi and come home now my darling," was all Richard was saying to me, in a weary kind of distressed tone.

When I finally got home and saw my husband unable to be seated for a few seconds before he got up and sat elsewhere, I was now convinced that something very dreadful had happened. He kept pacing and doing the same thing over and over. Something I never saw him done before.

"Honey, what is the matter?" I nervously asked my husband again.

He took a very deep breath then sharply announced that was a very fatal accident involving my family in St Thomas.

"Oh my God, oh my God, are they alright? Honey are they going to be okay?" I was losing my breath and trembling and crying at the same time. I could barely stand up. I held on to the arm of the sofa next to me for immediate support.

When my husband revealed to me that the authorities telephoned from St Thomas to inform that all of my loved ones lost their lives in a terrible road accident, I fainted instantly.

Three and a half hours later, I found myself in my bed, with my husband and a private nurse at my bedside. I recalled what my husband had told me before I fainted and began to weep. I had been given tranquilizers to calm me down. But I still couldn't come to terms with such very devastating news. My whole world had been crumbled right before my very eyes. How could I ever cope with the tragic loss of my precious six relatives at the same time. And in the horrendous manner in which they lost their lives. The more I think about it, the crazier I was becoming.

"How did it happen?" I asked my husband, wiping the tears from my eyes.

He said that the authorities told him that a bus with around eighteen passengers was found at the bottom of a cliff, killing seventeen of the passengers. The only survivor, was a nine month old baby , who was discovered beneath a seat of the bus, shielded by the body of his mother. I couldn't deal with such sad and unimaginable news. It was too much to bear.

Oh my God, why did you let such horrible accident took the life of so many of my loved ones? Why Lord?

I couldn't know the possible answers to the many questions I was seeking all at once. I wanted to die. I don't know if there would be a tomorrow for me. For just like that, my aunt and her husband along with my mother and younger siblings met such cruel death. I couln't imagine their desperate screams they made seeing their death before their eyes. Mother must have had a heart attack as would my aunt. How very painfully sad.

They were going on a tour around the island. I could imagine how excited they all were. My aunt must have cooked up a storm. They must have planned to have a very good day together. But now, all my thoughts were pure imagination. For there, my family lies in some morgue on ice, lifeless and lost hope in life.

> You saw the dark clouds that came,
>
> You heard the thunder cried their names.
>
> The rain poured down with grief

And the sun rose without steam.

Tell me, who wouldn't cry

As hope vanished before one's eyes?

Mother, aunt, uncle, my sisters, my brother,

You've met such a cruel disaster!

My husband has been my rock and support in the deepest and darkest moment in my life. It was ever more heart breaking when Andy learned of the tragic news. He kept calling back, wanting to know if he had had a bad dream. We both wished it had been a bad dream, but very unfortunately, it was not my brother.

Many members from my aunt's church were also calling, shocked by the news and offered their deepest sympathies to us. Pastor Joseph has been speaking with my husband about the funeral arrangements. He knew that I was in no frame of mind to assist. My burden was greater than any hurt I had ever felt

Sorrow overtakes me with a passion

Just thinking about my lost loved ones

It's not a dream. It's for real.

It's not a dream. It's for real!

177

My husband has been in touch with the authorities from St Thomas. They were going to send the bodies of my poor beloved loved ones on a private plane in a week's time. The U S government has also taken the responsibility of burying all the victims of the fatal accident. The accident was being reported on all radio and TV stations in the region and in the United States as well.

The bodies finally arrived on the island. I couldn't enter the mortuary. While my husband and a few others went to view the bodies, I stayed outside in the car and wept silently, knowing well that there won't be anymore phone conversations, no more visits and no more hopes for my mother, aunt, her husband, Jason, Samantha and Kizzy. They have gone to where my grandparents are. I prayed to the Lord that they all made it into heaven, for indeed, that is the only hope I have in seeing them again, in another life, whenever that time arrives for me.

Andy and his wife and their child, arrived a few days before the funeral. My poor brother and I hugged and cried over our loss. He wanted to see the bodies. My husband took him to the mortuary but I saw my poor brother running out, crying and vomiting. He said, "sis, what a terrible sight to see. They're almost unrecognizable." We both just stood outside the mortuary and cried floods of tears.

The funeral service was held at the church my aunt used to frequent. It was packed to capacity. There were also many onlookers outside of the church. There was such a sombre mood. It was indeed the worse day in my entire life.

The six coffins were brought into the church and were lined side by side. I wanted to faint, just looking at the surreal experience. I looked like a lost lamb who has lost its owner and

didn't know where to go. I couldn't cry anymore. I have cried so much since the dreadful news broke of my family that day. Now no more tear drops were falling from my eyes but I was literally dying inside. My husband was at my side and so were Andy, his wife and child. Andy, who was wearing dark shades, couldn't control the tears that kept falling down his face. My dear husband had one hand around my shoulders, trying to comfort me. I welcomed that, but it wasn't enough. The reality has not sunken in that I actually lost six family members in such a tragic bus accident. It was beyond my comprehension to think that with those coffins, were the crushed bodies of my mother, aunt, her husband and the rest of my siblings, going to their graves in very different forms; some with missing eyes and fingers, mangled faces, broken feet and ribs. Thinking of it has augmented my pain and suffering, much deeper. All I was thinking within my mind was about my poor loved ones and the abrupt and catastrophic end to their beautiful lives. No more life for all of them.

> No more, no more,
> My loved ones, no more.
> No more, no more.
> All gone, my beloved; no more!

The funeral service got on the way. I was too weak to even stand or sing. The congregation started singing, 'It is well with my soul...' There were outbursts of tears from many. The eulogy was most heart breaking. I began to cry and screamed but the strength of my voice was gone. But still, I cried all through the song, 'Through all the changing scenes of life,'.........come back to me, while my eyes continued to look with disbelief at the many people who turned out to pay their last respect to my lost six.

Pastor Joseph's sermon was sad and dreary. He too, was wiping tears from his eyes. "Someday, someday, in the sweet bye and bye, we'll understand it better. Someday, we hope to reunite with our friends and family in the heavenly skies. Cry now. Pour out your grief for I know how it feels to lose a loved one, much less to six at the same time." Pastor Joseph's sermon brought a hint of hope, comfort and sorrow to my bleeding heart.

At the graveyard, I couldn't bear to see my loved ones put to rest in their individual graves. I advised my husband to take me away from the site. Uncle Arthur and his brother Jim were there, also mourning the passing of the six. My brother was crying again . I felt dizzy. My stomach felt like it wanted to rip from within my body. My husband held on to me. I was losing it and scarcely could walk. A lady came by and whispered to me, "Don't cry my dear, it's gonna be okay, it's gonna be okay."

How could she ever tell me not to cry when her eyes were also filled with tears? My husband and I continued to walk away from the graveyard. The lady was following us too. She was now trying hard not to let me see her crying, but I did. She gently touched me on my shoulder and said, " Two years ago, I lost my only child and husband in a car accident and today, I'm still living with that sad memory." I couldn't reply. She understood. Before she left us, she gave my husband a sheet of paper on which she said has a poem, her and telephone number. As we continued to walk out the cemetery, I looked back, in direction at the burial site. The gravediggers were covering the last remains of my loved ones. I wanted to run back to the burial site to be buried with my loved ones but I had no energy. I couldn't. I looked at my husband and held on to him with a tighter grip. His eye red and looked as if he hadn't slept for days.

"Hon let's go home," he sadly said to me as he continued to hold on to me and led me to our car. While we drove back to our house, I became deeply attached to the significance of loss. I became involved with a great loss. I tried to forget my great loss but I couldn't. I have climed to familiar steps to face the inevitable news of more than one loved one lost. Such a mountain of loss!

When we got home, my husband fixed me a hot cup of chocolate. I hardly drank it. I had no appetite. Still he forced me to drink it because I had hardly eaten since I heard of that fatal accident that cruelly took away piece of my heart.

Quite a number of people showed up at our house after the burial. They came to comfort me. Their presence I didn't mind, but I felt totally disconnected from this life. I had no more joy in me. It had all been taken away and replaced with so much grief in my heart. Do you really know how it feels to lose a loved one? In my case, six. Do you know I can't sleep at nights? Do you know I've said every prayers I could possibly remember and still I feel totally lost? Do you feel my hurt, my pains, my fairs, my loss? What do you feel about death itself?

Any and his family brought uncle Arthur and Jim to the house. There was not time to think in that moment what uncle Jim had done to me in the past. Besides my husband, they were the only remaining immediate family I had and at such a difficult passage in our lives, we needed to stick together.

That evening, I was mentally drained and wanted to go to sleep but I couldn't. A few people , decided to stay the night with us. They weren't going to sleep but were there to try and make the atmosphere less tense, by playing cards, drinking rum and talking. I eventually drank a good portion of brandy in the hope I could fall asleep , knowing fully that the next day would still bring back reality and more sad memories.

Many continued to express their condolences. We have been receiving numerous phone calls practically every day. Each passing day, I asked the Lord to grant me the serenity to accept the things I could not change, courage to change the things I could and wisdom to know the difference. One morning, I'd wake feeling a bit optimistic about life , then the next morning and the day after, I'd wake up feeling pessimistic about life. My husband has been a continuing source of inspiration. He has been always optimistic and reassured me that he would help me to slowly get over such tragedy. He confessed too, that it wouldn't be easy but He couldn't afford to let the happiness we once had , die. His encouragement helped me to live one day at a time.

"Hon, do you know how much I share and feel your hurt?" he would ask every now and then, while giving me an embrace.

"I know you do darling, I know you do," was my calm response.

He would stress, "You're all I ever need and it hurts me way down to see you like that. Only my heart feels about you and your terrible loss. Be strong Bee, be strong. It's the only hope that'll keep us alive and well."

My husband was absolutely right about that. I must try to keep hope alive for both of us.

Sophie has also been very supportive. She is my best friend. She has spent a lot of time with me, reminding me how I always had a positive outlook on life and I should pray and continue to do so, however I can.

It wasn't easy to see Andy and his family boarded the aircraft. I kept saying in my mind that I wouldn't see them again, that something terrible would happen to them in Switzerland. And I couldn't deal with another loss like that. My brother was concerned about me too, but having realized the strong support my husband has been giving me, he praised my husband and felt somewhat assured that my husband will continue to look after me. Andy also promised that he would never break our line of communication by calling me at least once a week. I cherished that last hug and kiss I got from my only living sibling and wished him and his family all the very best. The parting was a very difficult one.

All of a sudden, I was afraid of the dark. I have been also having a lot of nightmares so I no longer sleep in the dark. There were many nights too that I woke from my sleep, crying from a bad dream. My husband would cuddle me and comforted me in his arms. Then I realized that I wasn't physically all alone.

A few months passed since my dear loved were put to rest. Many saw a different Belinda. Sophie and the other girls from the office would invite me and my husband to a few functions but never went, although we always promised possibly the next time.

One evening while Richard and I were lying in the bedroom, I mentioned to him that it would be a good idea if we plan to have our first child. My husband agreed right away. He thinks having a baby, would definitely ease some of the pain I was still feeling, over the catastrophic departure of my loved ones, from this life.

"You know, I've been thinking about that recently too and that's so good that you just brought it up," my husband replied with joy.

"I feel it would make things look a little livelier around the place, having a child to deal with," I added.

"And more fun if twins were to arrive!" Richard teasingly remarked.

"Oh no dear! No twins. Just one little boy or girl would do in the meantime," I quickly replied, almost sounding like I was on the defense.

"Agreed. One little boy or girl would be fine for us," Richard confirmed.

"And if it were just all about that 'mini snake and what it does' and what you often talk about , then my dear wife, you know it would be more than a baby boy or girl at once! Richard boldly mentioned without restriction. And that made me smiled. Something I have done in a long time.

"Oh Richard, you really are too much. Look what you're thinking, you little naughty you!" It forced me into laughter.

I became pregnant much sooner than I expected. Richard and I were really thrilled of the exciting news. All of a sudden, I was anxious to become a mother, to hold my baby for the first time, to look into his face and smile at our new miracle. The feeling was just indescribable. I was beginning to think that our baby would truly bring some well deserved happiness in our lives.

Just after four months in my pregnancy, Richard urged me to quit work. According to my husband, he didn't wish for me to be working hard. He wanted to be sure that I would get enough rest and eat well so that we'd have a healthy baby. My husband said over and over again that he just couldn't wait to be a father again.

Sophie suggested that I shouldn't just give up my job but request for some time off and once that was granted, then I would be entitled to maternity leave further in my pregnancy. After having spoken with my husband about that and he agreed, I considered Sophie's suggestion.

My manager also had compassion on me and expressed how I might have been feeling in the last couple of months, following the untimely death of my loved ones. I was now on unpaid leave, which would be followed by maternity leave.

Richard introduced me to a very nice doctor, whom he said, was his ex-wife's doctor during and after her pregnancy.

Dr Jackie Browne ran some tests on me, which was something normal for every pregnant woman under her care. Of all the tests, I hated taking blood. When the doctor pricked my vein for it, I almost cried out loud!"

"It's not that bad, Mrs Luke," The doctor softly remarked even she noticed the look on my face.

The doctor also suggested that I could take an ultrasound test in the near future to determine the sex of the baby if I wanted to.

My husband, although he didn't want to, had to travel again for his company. This time he would be gone for two weeks. Sophie's boyfriend was away on vacation. She didn't mind spending all that time at our house. I felt a bit better, knowing that there would be someone around, should I develop a sudden emergency with my pregnancy.

Richard left, not feeling too happy about that but it was an urgent matter for the company to which he has to represent. I also encouraged him to go and told him that I would be fine. He kissed me again told me to take care of the baby and myself. He assured me to that he would telephone me during the times he wasn't busy with work.

One mid afternoon, while I was in the kitchen preparing something to eat, the house phone rang and when I answered it, a woman with a Spanish accent said, "Ello, me warn to speaky wit Richar.."

I questioned who it was, but the lady gave no reply. Then the phone went dead for a few seconds, followed by an erratic tone. At first, I didn't think it was strange for some Spanish

woman to be calling our number asking for Richard. It could have been a coincidence. She might have wanted another person also called Richard, whether by first or last name.

But when the same woman called back later that day, I realized somehow, that she was dialling the right number. At the same time, I thought Richard might have given her the number to call to find out if I had any domestic chores for her to do. Or maybe he had spoken to one of his friends about getting me a maid because of my pregnancy. He's that type of man who would do everything to make me happy.

"Ello, Richar there?" asked the woman in a spanish accent.

"Richard who?" I asked

"Richard at workey in de company for painty," she replied.

She knew whom she was calling for. I wanted to know why this woman was calling for my husband. I didn't have the answers. All kinds of thoughts were now running through my mind. One that actually weighed heavily on my mind, was whether or not my husband had anything personally to do with this Spanish woman. To think that my husband might have cheated on me, disturbed me. There was no evidence, no clue whatsoever that he was sleeping around with any woman. And I never would have believed anyone wanting to spread such false rumours about my husband. In fact, I would consider suing that person who wants to damage my husband's reputation.

I repeated slowly to the Spanish woman that my husband wasn't around but she could leave her number so that he could call her back. She didn't have a home number or mobile phone. She was calling from a public phone booth but told me to tell my husband that Maria called.

When Sophie came by that evening, I related my telephone encounter with a woman called Maria.

" A Dominicana? Those bitches. I don't like them," my friend shamelessly admitted to me.

"By the way, what did she want, Belinda?"

When I let her know that she was calling for me husband, her composure changed.

"What's the matter Sophie?" I immediately asked.

"I just don't trust most of those women from the Dominican Republic. Can't you see how many of them are on this small island and what most of them are up to? Sophie quickly informed me.

Apparently, Sophie's former boyfriend used to frequent the brothels, unknown to her. When she eventually discovered his secret rendezvous, she said 'adios' to him. Since then she cannot stand most of those women from the Dominican Republic.

"They're too damn smart and lie, always looking for men that have money," Sophie further commented.

I couldn't wait for Richard to call home. When he did, I mentioned Maria.

"Oh, that must be my boss's maid," my husband informed me.

"I told her she should call you to find out if you wanted her to do anything around the house since you are heavily pregnant," my husband further disclosed to me.

I felt much better but still I was hoping that my husband was never involved with Maria or any other woman.

My husband mentioned that he was missing me and questioned about my growing stomach.

He was due to return home in a few days and I personally couldn't wait to see him again.

When I got off the phone with my husband, I suddenly realized that I didn't tell him that Maria didn't call about finding out if I needed her to do some work at home. She only asked for him, twice. I began to think that it would be a great idea to invite Maria over to the house, if she calls again, and pretended that I was Richard's sister in order to get some more relevant information from her. But she never called back. And I tried not to develop any headache about her telephone calls anymore.

Dr Browne called late one afternoon, around half past five and requested that I should come and see her right away. I was slightly panicking but asked if I could come to her office the next day. But she insisted I should come as soon as possible and not to panic. She knew my husband was away, so she didn't ask for him.

I drove my husband's car to Dr Browne's office in a jiffy. All of her staff had already left the office. I was becoming rather nervous again. She invited me into her office and told me politely to have a seat. Though she didn't show it on her face, she soon announced that there was some bad news from the different tests that she recently ran on me.

The next thing that came to my mind, maybe she discovered that my baby was growing abnormally inside my womb. Maybe she discovered that I have high blood pressure, severe diabetes. Or some ailment that she wanted to take care of as soon as possible to protect my unborn.

Dr Browne picked up a small white paper from a file and without much effort, softly announced that my blood test diagnosed me as being HIV positive. I felt a sudden sharp pain to the right side of my heart. I was completely shocked at that unexpected news. I didn't know what to say or do. But the tears began streaming down my face freely.

"No, no, this cannot be true, doctor. It's impossible, it's impossible," I screamed.

"I know how you feel, my dear friend, but I have had your blood sample tested four times from different labs and unfortunately, all read positive," the doctor revealed.

I wanted to die. I couldn't figure out how it happened. I have never cheated on my husband. I never had a blood transfusion and I couldn't figure out how it happened. Those were the thoughts that rushed through my head in that awful moment.

"Mrs Luke, I don't know what else to say, except I could offer you treatment, counselling and prayers. For, I couldn't believe myself when I saw the results," the doctor added.

She continued, "You and your husband appear to be so loving caring and caring for each other. I really don't know what to say plus I am not in any position to assume or cast judgement especially in my profession. But I was surprised when I saw the results," Dr Browne stated.

I wanted to leave the office and return home and hide myself in a room there and never come out from it. I pinched myself, to make sure that it was actually me, Belinda, sitting in the middle of a crisis. But it was me.

Dr Browne offered to let me stay with her for at least the night or to accompany me back to Luke's estate. But I refused both offers.

I eventually told the doctor I wanted to leave on my own and that I would take my time and drive slowly back to my residence. Before I left her office, she gave me a gentle tight squeeze and promised that she would be there to help me. She was also hoping to speak with my and husband and I soon, together.

I left the doctor's office with such a heavy burden with so much thoughts floating around in my head. My mind wasn't clear as to what or where I was heading to now. That news from the doctor has absolutely broken my heart. It was too much pain to bear. Jesus Christ!I drove into a gas station around after eight o'clock and fill tank of the car to capacity. I also purchased a bottle of brake fluid from the attendant. Drinking it was a great possibility.

"Why should I live with HIV when I didn't merit such illness?" I was talking loudly to myself and I drove and didn't know exactly where I was going. I thought about my poor innocent baby inside of me. I sobbed more when I realize the possibility that my baby may also be HIV positive. My poor baby didn't deserve that. I just don't wish for my baby to come into this world and suffer. Nor did I want to suffer this way.

I was still driving to no specific destination thinking too that my husband must have cheated on me and might have infected me with that deadly disease. Maybe that Maria who called the other day, had something to do with my husband sexually. Or my husband must have had several sexual encounters with other woman or women, who had already been infected with HIV and brought such incurable disease to me and my unborn angel. Please, Lord, I feel suicidal now. Please have mercy upon my distressed soul.

When would the madness of tragedy end? When would it cease? I had suffered so much before and now, when I was just having a share of happiness in my life, everything bad was now happening to me. I thought that my husband was my infinite source of happiness. Now I am angry for what state he has now put me and my baby in. I didn't deserve to die. Of course not!

I wanted to pull aside in the dark and drink all the brake fluid and just let my life go from this world. I didn't want to return to my own residence. I was poor Belinda again, with no one to call. No family, no friend, no husband.

When people discover that I have AIDS, they wouldn't want to be around me anymore. I've herd so many heart breaking studies of those with HIV, are often stigmatized and neglected by their own family and friends. Now that possibility has arrived at my own door.

As I continued to drive, I saw a tent filled with lights and people. I stopped to listen. They were singing, clapping and praising God. It looked like a church crusade. I wondered to myself if it would make any difference to my feelings, if I went in. I wiped my face again because the tears didn't seem to be in a hurry to stop falling! I didn't care what was going under the big tent, all I wished, was to walk straight to the altar there and pour out what's left of my heart to God. And hopes He hears me this time. I had no other alternative. I must try and work something out with the Lord. I need His blessings and healing. And I need it right away!

I parked my car and walked straight down the aisle to the altar under the tent and began praying and crying out to God, asking Him so many questions. The music and singing continued. I lifted my hands in the air, my eyes closed and wet with tears. I told the Lord that I didn't deserve to die this way. I begged Him to save me and my unborn, by healing us. I was talking to the Lord so much that I didn't realize that I was now all alone under the big tent. Everyone else apparently had left. Maybe the church service was close to ending when I got there or maybe nobody bothered with me, thinking I was a mad woman. I was caught up in my own sorrows that I was only concerned about getting healed. I continued to pray to the

Lord. I remembered when my grandma prayed for us and told us to have faith and patience in God. I now, wasn't in any hurry to leave the altar. No, I would continue to pour out my heart to the Lord, just like aunt Lyn had always encouraged me. For the only hope I truly had, was in Christ Jesus. He was the only hope to help me with my afflictions. I was also concentrating on Shirley Ceasar's song, 'Jesus is everything we need' and the part where she spoke... 'Even when the doctors send you home to die, say they can't do you no good, Jesus is going to be around your bedside, bringing healing when there's sickness. He is peace in the midst of a storm...'

Under the altar, I desperately waited for a reply from the Lord. I was waiting for a miracle!

EPILOGUE

Life (a mighty long road to travel on...)
By Belinda
Part 1 (As a little girl)
Call me Innocent,
Look at my face,
What do you see?
Can't you tell
That with me, life's
Not so well?
I represent the other children
Who are already learning
Day by day,
Who are already seeing
Night after night,
Their plight multiply,
Their hopes diminish.
The environment isn't good.
Children are being pushed
To the ground, only the
Strong would survive.
Like Belinda of Brookes,
Who's taking the shoving and the push,
Walk beside me, brothers and sisters
Let's fight on.
Let's continue to carry on,
Despite all the odds

Part 2 (As a teenager)

Still drying my tears,
The feelings are the same.
I start to see differently.
Walk beside me, brothers and sisters,
The struggles continue.
From now on, I'll mark you.
You're my very concerns,
I want you to accomplish
I want you to see success
I want nothing but the best.
Harder days are here.
Hunger finds the victim here.
Call me Innocent,
Look at my face,
What do you see?
Can't you tell?
That with me, life's
Still not so well?
But let's continue to move on.

Part 3: (Now a woman)

It's more than tears now
Looking back but carrying on.
I see better days are coming,
I know I'm not dreaming.
Some prayers been answered
Bringing us closer to the light.
We are no longer children,
A big change in our lives.
Let's encourage little ones
To walk beside us,
Let's give them hope.
We have struggled before
And it's not all o'er.
And like Belinda, we give advice:
Walk with courage in life
Despite all the odds.
Walk in the light,
Though it's a tough fight.
Walk with God's always,
He'd give you courage
Yes, walk there, continue.
Walk; walk towards the light!
Walk to it, if you can!

Printed by Amazon Italia Logistica S.r.l.
Torrazza Piemonte (TO), Italy

41977901R00121